MISSION: THIRD FORCE

In the late 1960s, the Cold War threatens the survival of mankind. To help keep the uneasy peace, a new group of mercenaries is born: known as Weapons Analysis and Research, Incorporated. Whilst WAR, Inc. does not supply fighting troops, it provides training, equipment, systems, advice and technical expertise . . . Now former major Peter Carthage leads his men into the hostile jungles of Bonterre to prevent the overthrow of its government by guerrillas — and the mysterious Third Force known only as 'X' . . .

MICHAEL KURLAND

MISSION: THIRD FORCE

Complete and Unabridged

LINFORD
Leicester

First published in Great Britain

First Linford Edition
published 2016

A catalogue record for this book is available
from the British Library.

ISBN 978–1–4448–2807–8

Published by
F. A. Thorpe (Publishing)
Anstey, Leicestershire

Set by Words & Graphics Ltd.
Anstey, Leicestershire
Printed and bound in Great Britain by
T. J. International Ltd., Padstow, Cornwall

This book is printed on acid-free paper

DEDICATION:

To CAROL HUNTER

'As hard as diamonds,
as soft as moonlight,
as warm as sunlight
and as cold as the space
between the Stars'

1

As the elevator sank in its concrete shaft beneath the farmland of central New Jersey, the sound of sirens became indistinct and then disappeared. The men in the elevator, all in the uniforms of various United States military services, talked softly among themselves.

The elevator came to a stop far underground, and slowly rotated on its axis as steel baffles automatically slid into place in the shaft above. The door opened, and the men hurried out into the domed concrete corridor. At the far end of the antiseptic-smelling, brightly lit corridor two guards stood in front of a massive, concussion-proof door.

The uniformed men were checked through the door by one of the guards, and one by one went through to the room beyond, where a man in civilian clothes showed them to seats — folding chairs set up along one wall of the huge room.

1

The room, two stories high with a balcony running around the wall at the level of the second floor, was painted an immaculate off-white. Brilliant indirect lighting flooded every corner. The hum of air conditioning provided a soft background noise to the quiet conversation.

Seven men sat around a large table in the center of the room. The table held a relief map of the United States and seven inset panels. Each panel contained a double row of push buttons, a telephone and what looked like an electric typewriter. On a dais at one side of the room, one man sat at a complex console desk overlooking the table. The wall opposite the dais held a world map centered on the United States. Above the map was a screen on which the printing from a constantly clattering teletype was flashed.

Over the hum of electronic equipment and air conditioning a precise voice spoke from a loudspeaker. With every sentence lights appeared or went out on one of the two maps.

As this last group of observers took their seats along the side of the room, a

2

hush settled, broken only by the loud-speaker voice, the air conditioner and the footsteps of the guards on the balcony.

'*Objects now penetrating area three,*' the loudspeaker stated. '*Trajectory estab-lished. Probable impact area grid coordinates 785 slash 919. This is approximately four miles southwest of Chicago Ground Zero.*'

A series of dotted lines on the wall map, lines that originated somewhere on the other side of the North Pole, lengthened further into northern Canada. One of the seven men around the table started push-ing buttons and typing instructions. On the table map the light that represented Chicago changed from green to amber. A series of pin-sized orange lights flashed into being around Chicago.

CHICAGO MISSILE SITES AT READY appeared on the teletype screen.

A red light on the telephone beside one of the men started blinking. He picked up the phone and listened for a moment. With the phone still cradled on his shoul-der, he started typing instructions on the machine in front of him.

'*Location of all known hostile submarines*

3

now being posted,' the loudspeaker announced. '*Hunt and kill teams are receiving assignments.*'

Some two hundred white dots appeared scattered through the Atlantic and Pacific Ocean areas of the wall map. About fifty of the dots had red rings around them. On the information board in one corner of the map the notation 'white lights — submarines . . . red rings — missile-carrying submarines' appeared.

'*Atlantic pickets report nine — repeat, nine — objects on trace,*' the loudspeaker voice droned. And then, almost without a break, '*Six traces reported northern Pacific.*'

A bank of digital tape recorders along the wall opposite the observers clicked on. A panel above the tape recorders lit up with the words FILE ACCESS; and then: DATA RECOVERED; and then: PROCESS, one after the other, in no discernible order, fast enough so that the words seemed to flicker.

'*Atlantic report confirmed.*' Nine lines appeared on the wall map, passing over Norway and into the Atlantic Ocean.

4

The man at the console put on a telephone headset and spoke into it constantly while operating the knobs and switches on the control board in front of him. The men around the table were engaged in the sort of highly organized confusion that is the result of each man knowing his job perfectly and doing it at top speed. The observers at the side of the room sat quietly, each caught up in the spell of the scene before him and the web of his own thoughts. Now the action was proceeding too fast for any one man to follow.

75 PERCENT DEFENSIVE FORCES AT RED ALERT ALREADY.

'Atlantic objects impact areas established. All are East Coast priority one targets, with no overlap. List is now being posted.'

A complex pattern of lights grew on the two maps.

MISSILE ORIGIN POINTS ESTABLISHED AS VLADIVOSTOK AND URKUTZ COMPLEXES.

'Chicago intercept launch.'

EAST COAST MISSILE SITES AT READY 93 PERCENT.

'*Chicago down*,' the loudspeaker voice announced laconically. The first red light blinked on the table map.

EXECUTIVE PRIORITY PLAN NUMBER 1 COMPLETED.

This was the code term that notified the room that the President of the United States and his top advisors were now at a command post inside a high-flying jet. The location of this jet was unknown.

'*West Coast object track has established trajectory, target pattern top six on Western priority list. Now being posted.*'

'Attention please!' a voice boomed over a different loudspeaker. 'We can now confirm that Congress has declared that a state of war now exists in the United States. Coded confirmation follows.'

The teletype suddenly came to life: RETALIATION ORDER EXECUTED — PLAN C PLAN C PLAN C.

A new wave of lights covered the west-central area of the United States on the wall map. Dotted trace lines appeared from these lights to points inside the Soviet Union. As the missiles represented by these lights approached their targets, the dotted traces would turn solid to show their progress. One by one green markers appeared on the ocean sections of the wall map. These represented the American missile submarines, each position being posted as the ship reported in.

'*New trace patterns on West Coast radar. Believed to be manned bombers.*'

The light that marked New York City turned red. A second later Washington and Boston were also red.

'*Manned bombers confirmed.*'

INTERCEPT FLIGHTS 10TH AND 114TH SQUADRONS AIR DEFENSE COMMAND NOW AIRBORNE.

SAC PRIMARY WAVE GIVEN GO CODE. SECONDARY WAVE NOW AIRBORNE.

'*On information received,*' the loud-speaker voice announced, '*Soviet ground forces are advancing into Germany. Berlin is still holding. NATO command has assumed control of all allied forces in Europe.*'

PHASE ONE COMPLETE, the teletype announced.

Suddenly the humming sound stopped. All the lights on the two maps went out.

'May I please have your attention,' a new voice asked over the loudspeaker. 'What you have just witnessed is Phase One of an operational test exercise we call 'Operation Lastday.' The enemy forces were simulated by a preprogrammed computer. The response of our command room was taped, and is now being fed into a computer for analysis. The results will be available in a short time.

'The room you are in is set up according to a system we call 'Group Control Command,' or G.C.C. We feel that it offers several advantages over the one presently in use. Brochures will be made available upstairs in the green room, along with a full explanation of what you have just seen, and coffee and doughnuts. These brochures are classified Top Secret, and will not leave the building.

'War, Incorporated, thanks all of you for your interest and cooperation.'

2

Colonel Lyet rode in his staff car at the head of the supply column. 'When commanding native troops,' read one of his doctrines, 'always do it from the front rather than the rear; it gives them confidence.' Colonel Lyet considered the men under his command 'native troops,' although he himself had been born in a village no more than forty miles from his present headquarters. The colonel had attended military schools and Staff College in France, and he carried their precepts and doctrines as frontlets before his eyes. It never occurred to him that techniques developed for warfare on the plains and hedgerows of France might not be valid in the jungles of Bonterre. Colonel Lyet, in all fairness, had held a staff position in the training college in Bonterre, capital city of the country of Bonterre, since the French had left his country. This was his first jungle command.

Colonel Lyet was engaged in one of his favorite sports: lecturing the junior officers in the staff car. The lecture was on one of Bonterre's newest phenomena: the guerrilla. Lyet, who had not as yet even seen a guerrilla, fondly assumed that this was because they were afraid of him.

'The guerrilla is a coward,' Colonel Lyet pronounced. 'He fights best at night, he will only attack a force inferior to his own, he fades into the bush at the first sign of serious resistance; he refuses to meet any regular Army force in open combat . . . '

'But Colonel,' interrupted a lieutenant who had actually read Mao Tse-tung's book on guerrilla warfare, 'could these traits not be considered as a form of prudence rather than cowardice? In what Mao Tse-tung calls the 'second phase' of the guerrilla war, it is essential . . . '

Colonel Lyet snorted. 'Second phase, indeed. How can one separate the actions of a group of bandits into phases? The guerrillas are cowards, it's as simple as that. If they weren't, they'd come out and fight like men instead of skulking around in the jungle.'

Somewhere, off to the left of the command car, a whistle blew.

'What — ' the colonel started.

There was the sudden sound of an explosion behind them.

'Stop the car,' Colonel Lyet snapped to his driver. He jumped out while the car was still moving, and ran toward the rear of the column. His three junior officers raced to catch up.

The earth suddenly dropped out from under Colonel Lyet's feet, and a wall of air hit him between the shoulder blades, throwing him face-first into the mud by the side of the road. The colonel reflexively kept rolling and dropped into a shallow ditch off the road.

He pushed himself to a sitting position and shook his head to clear it. Lieutenant Twom, the reader of Mao Tse-tung, was crawling toward him. The lieutenant's right leg was soaked with his own blood.

The staff car, a crumpled wreck behind the lieutenant, made a *churking* sound and burst apart, sending up a sheet of

11

flame. The other two officers lay in grotesque positions on the road.

The lieutenant rolled into the ditch with Colonel Lyet. 'What happened?' he asked. 'A mortar shell?'

Lyet took the bright yellow kerchief from around the lieutenant's neck and started to tourniquet the bleeding leg. 'No, it was a land mine. We're being ambushed with great finesse.'

'Notice, sir, it's on a main road, less than sixty kilometers from the capital. What does this do to your coward theory?' The lieutenant grimaced with pain. 'And in broad daylight, too.'

'Bah!' Colonel Lyet finished adjusting the tourniquet. 'Skulking in the jungle like macaques. It's a very clever ambush. I said they were cowardly, not stupid.'

The sound of machine-gun fire approached, and a squad of Bonterre soldiers ran down the road toward where the colonel squatted. The men darted from truck to truck, pausing to fire to their rear as they ran. Colonel Lyet waved to the group. One of them started at this sudden motion from the side of the road and raised his rifle, but the sergeant knocked it aside before the error was compounded.

The soldiers, one at a time, separated from the cover of the trucks, ran the short distance across the road, and dived into the ditch holding the colonel and Lieutenant Twom.

Colonel Lyet counted the men as they came across. The sergeant, who came last, was number sixteen.

'Can you tell me what happened?' Lyet asked the sergeant.

'I'm not sure, sir. I was in the first truck that carried troops,' the sergeant said, breathing deeply. 'The truck in front of ours was blown up. We jumped off of our truck, and the machine guns started in. They had us in a crossfire. I dived under the truck. A lot of the men didn't make it, but some, I think, made it to the woods.'

'What of the men in the rear trucks?'

'We were cut off, sir, I don't know.'

The machine-gun fire started up again, somewhere just out of sight. Colonel Lyet spread the men around the ditch, facing out toward the unseen enemy. He put the injured lieutenant in the most protected position he could find in one corner of the long, muddy hole.

Staring off into the jungle, Colonel Lyet tried to decide what to do next. All he could think of, was that his force of 240 men had been cut down to sixteen in one blow. *I put all my men in the rear trucks, so if we were attacked I could outflank them*, Lyet thought bitterly. *Very clever! They hit exactly where the men were. How the hell did they find out?*

He smashed his closed fist against the other palm. 'How the hell did they know?' he muttered.

'Sir?' The sergeant looked up from his rifle.

'Nothing, Sergeant, nothing. Keep a sharp lookout.'

A machine gun rattled in the brush. It sounded quite close to them. There was a sharp scream, and then silence. The men fidgeted and kept glancing all around. They seemed close to panic. *What can I do?* Colonel Lyet wondered. *I'm close to panic myself. How can you expect men to fight something they can't even see?*

The machine gun sounded again, this

time from right on top of them. One of the men shuddered, and went rigid. He made a gagging sound as he fell, blood pouring out of his nose and mouth.

Something snapped inside the colonel's head. He started shaking the sergeant. 'Shoot, man, for the love of God, shoot!'

'At what?' the sergeant yelled. He slapped Colonel Lyet across the face. The colonel went rigid with anger, and then slumped down in the ditch. 'Thank you, Sergeant,' he said.

The machine gun sounded again, short staccato coughing noises that filled the jungle. Another gun joined the chorus. Bullets poured into the ditch. The huddled men started firing back at the enemy they couldn't see. One of the soldiers screamed briefly, and then choked, falling back in the ditch.

Colonel Lyet stood up and pulled at the flap of his holster. Machine-gun bullets splintered the tree to his left, and a wood chip cut the colonel's cheek. The colonel got his pistol free of the holster, and worked the slide. 'Cowards,' he yelled, firing into the screen of trees in front of him, 'come out and fight, goddam you!' He felt a sharp pain in his shoulder, and then he was plunging forward into nothing.

3

Weapons Analysis and Research, Incorporated, spread its substantial acreage over a hill in northern New Jersey. It was a young company, its existence brought about by a political situation unique in history. The initials of the company name spelled WAR, and war was its only business.

In less mechanized times its employees might have donned armor, ridden horses, carried long pikes and called themselves *condottieri:* freelance soldiers, owing allegiance only to the prince who paid them. But times change, and modem mercenaries don't resemble their ancestors any more than modern weapons resemble pikes.

The large bloc of so-called neutral countries, although doing their best to remain uncommitted in the power struggle between East and West, usually had military or paramilitary problems of their own. Calling for aid and advice from one of the larger powers was considered a sign of picking sides. If Ruritania asks for military aid from the U.S.S.R., headlines would read:

RURITANIA RECEIVES RUSSIAN MILITARY ADVISORS, COMMUNIST ALIGNMENT SEEN NEAR.

If, on the other hand, Ruritania asks the United States for assistance, the headlines would say:

RURITANIA SEEKS U.S. AID AND MILITARY ASSISTANCE IN ANTI-COMMUNIST STRUGGLE.

Chances are that Ruritania only wants to modernize its small army to put down a rebellion of tribes near the Northern border, tribes possibly being secretly aided by a neighboring 'nonaligned' country. Small nations have their own problems.

And so, to meet the modern needs generated by the Cold War a modern group of mercenaries was born. WAR, Inc., did not supply fighting troops. It did supply training, equipment, systems, advice and technical know-how for using the equipment of modern warfare. Its men were carefully-selected experts at their jobs.

*   *   *

Peter Carthage stood in the middle of the green room and checked off the names on his list. 'Major Marion,' he called. A short, balding U.S. Army major hurried over to join the group.

'You're the last one,' Peter told the major. He addressed the six men standing around him. 'Good afternoon. My name is Peter Carthage, and my official title here is Expediter. I have no better idea of what that title means than you do.

'I hope you've enjoyed the display we put on for you downstairs. While the others stay here for coffee and critique, you gentlemen are invited to take a guided tour of the facilities and grounds. If you'd care to join me, I think you'll find it interesting.'

'Why us in particular?' an Army colonel asked.

'I couldn't tell you,' Peter said. 'For

19

some reason the Old Man has decided to impress you — or, at least, try to impress you.'

Carthage had a good idea why these men were chosen. It was probably the same sort in recruiting effort that had got him into the company two years before. These men had skills that War, Inc., thought it could use.

War, Inc., was growing, slowly and carefully, but still growing. Since the company depended for its existence on the knowledge, skill and abilities of its employees, new positions were filled very carefully.

Up until two years ago, Peter had been a major in the Intelligence branch of the United States Army. He had been recommended for the job with Weapons Analysis and Research, Inc., by an ex-colonel friend who was head of Plans Division for War, Inc.

Thomas Steadman, the 'Old Man,' President of War, Inc., had called Peter in for an interview. Each man liked what he saw. Peter Carthage was now one of three men in the company holding the title of Expediter. The job had a wide range.

Over the two years he had been with the firm he had helped to research reports on everything from the effective blast radius of the new 'baby' hydrogen warheads to the danger of tetanus infection from the dung-tipped bamboo stakes guerrillas are so fond of leaving as booby traps.

Peter sometimes regretted the lack of physical excitement, but the firm disapproved of any but necessary participation in the various subjects they did research on.

Peter escorted his guided tour group out of the green room and across a lawn that would be the envy of any college campus. He stopped in front of a low gray building.

'Personnel Weapons Branch,' he explained to the group. 'Affectionately known by us as the department of dirty tricks.' He pressed a button beside the steel door.

A small slit appeared in the top of the door. 'Bulletproof mirror,' Peter commented, pointing. 'Gentlemen, you're now on television.'

After a short pause, a man in a white smock opened the door. 'This is Doctor

Anderson,' Peter introduced. 'He'll show off our latest collection of nasty toys for all those as are interested.'

Doctor Anderson, a short, balding man with circular eyeglasses, gave a hearty chuckle as he shook hands with the members of the group. 'Toys for boys of all ages,' he said, 'but to be treated with respect; some of them are indeed quite nasty.' He led his audience into the building.

The group stood at one end of a wide corridor, with many doors leading off from both sides. Doctor Anderson took them to a door on the right. Over the portal a white sign said 'Laboratory #3 — No Entrance When Red Light Is On.' The red light, mounted on the left side of the entrance, was off.

'The first thing I'd like to show you,' Anderson said as he escorted them into the room, 'is our new perfected model of the World War Two OSS hand grenade.' Inside the door, and past the concrete explosion-proof screen, the group gathered around a heavy metal table.

'I didn't know there was an OSS

grenade,' an Army major commented.

'It didn't see much use,' Anderson explained, 'as a matter of fact, it was junked right after its first public demonstration.'

'Oh, really?' The major was interested.

'Yes. You see, it was a contact grenade. An OSS agent in occupied France happened to be on the side of a mountain with a group of *Maquis* people when a German convoy passed below. He thought this would be a great opportunity to take out the convoy. He had his group toss grenades — the conventional four-second fuse types — over the side of the mountain. Most of the grenades bounced harmlessly off the German vehicles and further down the cliff before they exploded. The Germans took out most of the Resistance group, including the OSS man. When word of this reversal got back to Washington, they decided to develop a grenade that would go off on contact for use in similar circumstances. The lab boys came up with a grenade that was completely safe to handle but, if thrown over thirty feet, would explode the moment it touched. The thirty feet was the distance it took the grenade to arm itself.'

'Did it work?' the major asked.

'Oh, yes,' Anderson assured him.

'Then, what went wrong?'

'Yes,' Peter asked, leaning against the table, 'you have us fascinated. What happened?'

'Well, Mister Carthage, it's a case in point for the importance of proper training. OSS decided to demonstrate their new toy to a group of high brass, but somehow the demonstrator didn't get the point of all the careful lectures he'd had on the proper use of his deadly little baseball. Incidentally, the grenade looked and weighed about the same as a regulation hardball; the lab boys thought it would be more natural to throw something that looked and weighed — '

'Yes, yes,' Peter said, 'and?'

'Well, after assuring the assemblage that the contact grenade was safe until thrown over thirty feet, the demonstrator tossed it in the air and caught it again to prove his point.' Doctor Anderson gestured in demonstration. 'The demonstrator made one small mistake,' he said. 'Unfortunately, he happened to toss the grenade fifteen feet straight up. It came fifteen feet down, and, by the simple law of addition, blew the demonstrator to a plane of existence more tolerant of mistakes.'

'That was the end of the project?' a colonel asked.

'The whole idea was immediately scrapped,' Anderson agreed.

'But you've revived it?' asked the major.

'Improved it, I like to think,' Anderson said. 'Here, see for yourselves.' He pulled a metal box from under the table and, setting it down carefully in the middle of the table, opened it. It held several yellow baseball-like objects. He picked up one and held it out for inspection. A small globular projection held a ring and a curved handle. 'The ring is for attaching to belts or straps,' Anderson explained, 'and the handle, as on a standard grenade, is a safety switch. After the pin is pulled the grenade is still quite safe until the handle is released. The handle is spring-loaded, and will fly off by itself if the grenade is thrown.

'Normally the grenade operates with the standard four-second time-delay fuse, as for example — ' Anderson casually pulled the pin and dropped the grenade on the table. There was a tinging sound, as the spring tossed the safety handle across the room, arming the grenade.

Seven men reflexively dived for cover. Peter found himself crouched under the steel table with Major Marion.

A sharp cracking noise, as of a gunpowder cap going off, blended in with the sound of Doctor Anderson laughing. 'I should apologize for not telling you that it was only a demonstration grenade,' the doctor said.

The group climbed out from the various objects they were under. 'Yes,' the colonel said, examining the ruined crease in his dress trousers, 'I rather think you should.'

'I do, I do; and I commend you all on your excellent reflexes. Now — here's the interesting feature on this little gizmo.' Anderson took out another grenade and pointed to a red tab by its handle. 'When you pull this out,' he demonstrated by doing so, 'the grenade becomes a contact-detonating type. It's still safe, of course, until the pin is pulled out and the handle released. It's not, however, meant to play catch with.' Doctor Anderson pulled the pin and allowed the handle to spring away. 'Watch,' he said. He tossed the grenade gently toward the table. When it hit, the cracking sound was repeated

'That was the primer charge blowing,' Anderson explained. 'If that gadget were loaded with high explosive it would have an effective destruction radius of twenty-five feet. It can also be manufactured in thermite, concussion and gas types — this one would have carried a shrapnel load. Are there any questions?'

Peter looked around.

'No,' Major Marion answered for the group. 'It was very interesting.'

'Fine, fine.' Doctor Anderson rubbed his hands together. 'If you'll come this way, please.' He led the way down the corridor to another laboratory. White-smocked men were busy in the room doing precise things in a knowledgeable manner. Anderson took the group to an area on one side of the room.

'This is work area one,' he told his guests, 'we call it the playground. It's used for preliminary experimentation. When one of the staff gets an idea, we play with it here first to see if it merits a work number. If it gets a work number, we're obliged to develop it until it's either adopted or officially dropped.'

'Where do you get your ideas?' one of the group asked.

'Oh, a variety of places. We're always open to suggestions. Sometimes one of our own boys comes up with something, sometimes someone else in the firm has a brainstorm. Fairly often one of the men in Plans or Training will bring in a requirement for a certain result, and it's up to us to figure out how to get there from here.

'One thing we do have here that's fun and tends to be productive — war games.'

'War games?' the colonel asked.

'The front office calls them 'Operational Exercises,' but we call them war games. Once a month Training Section

runs a problem that all sections partici-
pate in. Our job in to develop equipment
that would be helpful.'

'What sort of equipment?'

'Could be almost anything.' Anderson
went over to a metal cabinet and started
fishing around.

After a few moments he dug out an
aerosol can. 'This gunk, for instance. The
serial number on the tag shows that it was
made up for the last exercise, about three
weeks ago.'

'What is it?'

'I don't really know, but I'll find out.'
Anderson checked the tag. 'Gummer!' he
called.

One of the white-smocked men across
the room dog-trotted over to the group.

'Gentlemen, this is Gummer. Gummer,
our guests are interested in the contents
of this can. What's in it?'

'Red paint,' Gummer replied.

The colonel laughed. 'What's so special
about a spray can of red paint?' he asked.

'Well,' Gummer took the can and held
it gingerly. 'This isn't ordinary red paint.'

'How so?' Doctor Anderson asked, with

an air of infinite patience.

'Thought of it during the last exercise,' Gummer explained. 'Part of the problem was airdropping supplies to a group deep inside of enemy territory. The drop area had to be marked for the planes, and then the markings had to be removed so that enemy troops couldn't find the area. The standard way is to use strips of white canvas, which have to be laid out to mark the drop zone and then rolled up and taken away. *I* thought of this.' He waved the cannister in the air.

'May I see it?' Peter asked.

'Certainly, Mister Carthage.' He handed the can to Peter and stood by like a small boy waiting for approval.

Peter examined the can carefully. 'Have you anything I can spray it on?' he asked Doctor Anderson.

'Oh,' Gummer said, 'you can spray it on anything you like. Here, I'll show you.' He took the can back from Peter and started to spray. He sprayed a strip on the floor and up one wall. The paint, a light, brilliantly fluorescent red, came out of the can in a fine mist. Gummer sprayed his own spotless rubber smock until it was mostly red, and then, as an afterthought, he grinned broadly and sprayed a red stripe from Doctor Anderson's right shoe up to his left shoulder.

Dr. Anderson, who looked like an over-zealous Croix-de-guerre winner ready for a Veterans' Day parade, was frozen speechless. With a great effort, he relaxed; keeping his hands carefully at his side. 'Gummer,' he said softly, 'this stuff better come off easily, or . . .'

Gummer snorted. 'Easily,' he said. 'Of course it comes off easily. Doesn't anybody listen when I explain something? Sometimes I think —'

'Gummer! Your basic problem is that most of the time you *don't* think. Remove the paint.'

Gummer went to the shelf and grabbed a small glass vial with a wax seal across the top. He ran his fingernail around the rim of the seal. The pungent odor of ammonia wafted from the vial and filled the room. Within seconds the brilliant red paint had turned into a fine white powder. The slight breeze of the air conditioning system lifted the powder and sucked it into the exhaust vents in the ceiling.

'It's not quite perfected yet,' Gummer said. 'There's a bit of the powder that you're going to have to brush off.'

'It's good enough,' Doctor Anderson said. 'Consider yourself redeemed.' Gummer smiled, nodded to the men, and wandered off back across the room.

'Well, I think we've taken up enough of your time, Dr. Anderson,' Peter said. 'We'll continue with our tour and let you get back to your work now.'

'It's been a pleasure,' Anderson said, shaking hands with the members of the guided tour.

As they made their way across the campus to the next point of interest, the major turned to Peter. 'You're certainly an informal group,' he said.

'We're all of that,' Peter agreed. 'It's a small company, and we find that we work better with an absolute minimum of red tape.' He paused in front of a small brick building.

'We might as well make this our next stop,' he said. 'This is the oldest building on the grounds. It was the only one here when War, Inc., bought the land. Legend has it that it was the administration building of an insane asylum that used to be here. We use it as our museum.'

As they rounded the corner of the building, they came face-to-face with a tank that appeared to be guarding the front door.

'Say,' the colonel said, 'I might be mistaken, but isn't that a Soviet T-34?'

'You're not mistaken, Colonel. It's a part of the museum.'

'Since when,' the colonel inquired, 'have the Russians started giving away their tanks?'

'That tank,' Peter waved grandiloquently, 'is a sign of the growing success of War, Inc.'s policies. It was one of a shipment to a small foreign power. With the tanks, Russia also sent a training program. The country in question soon made the surprising discovery that the training the Russians had in mind included a course in tactics.'

'Of course,' the major commented.

'Yes,' Peter said, 'you'd think so. But there was a slight difference in emphasis on the word 'tactics.' You might call their course 'Political Internal Subversion 304.''

'I see,' the major said.

'Well, when the government of the country found out, they kicked the Soviet training mission out of the country. They were then stuck with a supply of Russian tanks, and no one to teach them how to use them. It was suggested that they request aid from the United States, but there were two problems. First, these were, after all, Russian tanks. They somehow didn't think it would be proper. Second, they were afraid the American government might also wish to include a course in political orientation.'

'That's unfair,' the colonel protested. 'It's been the policy of the United States Government to refrain from interfering in the internal affairs of other countries.'

'Possibly, Colonel,' Peter said, 'but you might get an argument in some places about that. Anyhow, right or wrong, that's what this government thought. We were able to convince them that War, Inc., was impartial. They hired us, and we ran a tank-training school for six months. It worked out very well. The only trouble is going to come when they run out of spare parts for their tanks: I somehow don't think the Russians are going to be too cooperative about supplying more.'

'You do much business with foreign countries?' the major asked.

'We're trying to. We feel that they have to have some alternate to the present three or four 'big powers.' Most of our business is still consulting to the United States government, but last year we managed to do thirty-five percent of our business with small countries.'

Peter took the group inside of the museum building. 'Every exhibit is pretty well described by the identifying card,' he told them, 'so I won't have to lecture you. If you have any questions let me know. I probably won't be able to answer them myself, but I'll know who to ask.'

The group spread out to examine the various lugged exhibits in the oak-panelled room. One of them, an Air Force captain, paused to examine a ship model in a glass case.

'You like that?' Peter asked. 'You're

looking a scale reproduction of our navy.'

'Your navy?'

'All one ship of it. It's an old destroyer that we use for training and testing equipment. I understand the Old Man's thinking of doubling the size of the navy — he's been offered a chance to buy a World War Two fleet-type submarine, but he hasn't decided yet.'

The door to the museum opened, and a short-cropped head appeared in the doorway. When the owner of the head saw that the room was occupied by the group he was looking for, he came in. 'Peter,' he said, 'I've been looking for you. The Old Man wants to see you right away. I've been asked to take over the rest of the tour for you.'

'Right,' Peter said. 'Gentlemen,' he addressed his six escortees, 'I've been called by Doctor Steadman, our boss. This is John Little, he'll take my place as official guide.'

He introduced the six men to John, and then left the building.

4

The District VII Military Hospital occupied the whole third floor of the cinder block headquarters building of Bonterre's crack Third Paratroop Battalion. From the window of his private room Colonel Lyet, strapped and wired into his bed like some life-size marionette, had an excellent view of Fort Dryfus, from the cleared strip of land ten yards past the wire fence on his left, to a similar cleared strip on his right.

Directly in front of his window, past the Motor Pool garage, the Headquarters Company arms room and the Military Police squadron — all one-story wooden structures — Lyet could see the main gate, exit to the dirt road that led to Bonterre Highway number two: main road to the capital some 140 miles away.

Very few of the men in the Third Paratroop Battalion had ever flown in an airplane, much less made a qualifying jump with a parachute; the word 'para-troop' in the battalion title was an honorific, showing how good the Army thought the battalion was. It was good for morale: the men in the battalion wore their parachute insignia patch on their left shoulder with great pride.

Colonel Lyet, who quickly developed a distaste for watching the fluid drip into his vein from the bottle on his left while the bottle on his right filled up with liquids drained from his wounds, spent most of his time staring out his window. Watching the complex activity of daily life in the Army camp spread out below him kept his mind off the fact that he was one of 27 survivors in the 240-man convoy he had led.

Colonel Dodroy, commander of the Third Paratroop Battalion, and one of the few qualified paratroopers in the Bonterre Army, came up to see Lyet almost every morn-ing. They were old friends, having gone to Staff College in France together.

'The doctors say another week and they can unwire you from all these contrap-tions,' Dodroy had told him that morning.

'That'll be a blessing. You never realize how wonderful it is to be able to scratch an itch until that privilege is taken away from you.'

'As soon as that cast is taken off and you can hold a book, I'll bring you something to read so you can stop staring out of that blasted window.'

'It's not so bad,' Colonel Lyet said. 'I spent all morning watching that convoy come in and unload. I'm glad to see that some of them manage to get through.'

'That was a special convoy,' Dodroy told him. 'We didn't give the guerrillas' informer network a chance to work. The convoy was assembled and started in under half an hour. Did you notice the large packing crates that came out of the first three trucks?'

'You mean the ones that were put in the Headquarters Company arms room?'

'Them's the ones. They contain the hardware for the radio communications net we've been trying to get out here for the past year. With the command radio here, and out-stations at every village and outpost for fifty miles, we should be able to stop guerrilla activities in the area almost before they start.'

'It sounds very good,' Colonel Lyet commented, 'I hope it works.'

'It's not the final answer by a long way, but it's a good substantial first step.' Colonel Dodroy picked up his hat from the table by the bed. 'I've got to get back to work. Madame DuMarte is due to visit the post in ten minutes to discuss precautions she can take against guerrilla raids. If there's anything I can do for you, let me know.'

'DuMarte?'

'Big plantation owner. Her land stretches from outside the fort to the ocean. The guerrillas haven't bothered her yet, and we're trying to keep it that way.'

'Ah! Mustn't keep the lady waiting.'

'I wouldn't think of it.' Colonel Dodroy smiled. 'Besides being one of the biggest landowners in the country, Madame DuMarte is very attractive.' He left the room.

From his window vantage point Colonel Lyet kept a close watch on the Fort's activities for the rest of the day.

As the evening slowly turned into night, the Fort settled down. The men had their evening meal of rice and fish, and retired to the barracks to attend to housekeeping chores and then sleep. The floodlights around the perimeter fence were turned on, and the guard mount was posted for the night.

Colonel Lyet relaxed and tried to go to sleep. Without the distraction of activity in the world outside his window, his thoughts kept returning to the ambush.

Two hundred forty men, he kept thinking, and only twenty-seven left. They must have known which trucks the men were in, that's the only answer. How? How could they have known? How did they know? The question tormented him, and he was unable to sleep.

Deprived by his cast of even the solace of tossing about in his bed, Colonel Lyet found that he was wide awake, his eyes open and staring at the ceiling. He turned to the window to watch the measured tread of the guard by the fence as a soothing substitute to counting sheep.

Lulled by watching the distant guard, the colonel had almost drifted to sleep, when his eye was caught by a flicker of movement in the jungle beyond the fence. He was suddenly completely alert and watching. For a while nothing happened; then, further along the fence, there was a brief scurry of motion. A man appeared at the edge of the jungle, ran halfway across the ten-yard cleared strip and then dropped. The guard completed his march in the other direction, and turned around to come back. He, apparently, was unable to see anything wrong beyond the fence perimeter. With slow, measured steps he paced by the spot where the figure was lying prone on the grass.

Colonel Lyet, prevented by the cast on both arms from reaching the call button, yelled to attract the attention of a nurse. No one answered his call, and he was forced to watch impotently as the rest of the drama unfolded.

★　★　★

Thombo Quat, captain in the Bonterre People's Volunteer Rebel Army, slowly crawled to the edge of the clearing and surveyed the ten-yard strip that separated his jungle hiding place from the fence surrounding Fort Dryfus.

A short, squat man with the sinewy grace of years of living in the jungle, Captain Quat was completely silent as he peered cautiously about the floodlit area. He first located his objective, and noted the spot in the wall of jungle closest to it; and then timed the march of the guard, watching for three cycles to make sure there was little deviation.

When he had established these facts, he faded back into the jungle as quietly as he had appeared.

Some yards back, two men were waiting for him in a small hollow.

'Well?' one of the men whispered. 'It is good. Be very quiet and follow me.' Captain Quat led the way through the darkened jungle underbrush. The two men, one of them with a small, wooden box strapped to his back, followed closely.

'We're almost at the clearing,' Captain Quat's soft whisper floated back to the men. They went a few yards further on, and then Quat hissed, 'Drop!' The three guerrillas lay on their stomachs, looking out into the glare of the floodlights.

'Tern, look closely. The wooden building directly across the clearing is your target. I've timed the guard. You'll have to make the run to the fence in two parts. When I tap you on your back, start running. Keep down low. When you're halfway across the clearing, drop flat.

'The guard will be at the far end of his post, off to your right. Wait five seconds before looking up — he'll be the most alert as he makes his turn. After another twenty seconds he should be even with you. If you make no sound, he will not turn around, so you'll be able to make it to the fence then. This will be the dangerous part. You'll have to lie by the fence as the guard passes, and he'll be no more than three feet from you. You must become part of the ground.'

'I understand.'

'Of course. You have the wire cutters?'

Tern produced an old but well-oiled pair of wire cutters from beneath his tattered shirt.

'Fine. Phom, give me the bomb.'

44

The third member of the expedition released the strap that held the wooden box to his back, and handed the box carefully to Captain Quat. Quat opened the top of the box, fed a string through a hole in the side, and then closed and sealed the top.

'Tern,' the captain whispered, 'plant this as close as you can to the rear of the building, and then pull this string out until you hear a click. You will then have four minutes to get away. If you make it without being seen, return to this spot; if anyone spots you, just try to make it to the jungle.'

'Very good, my captain. For the glory of the people.'

'The glory of the people, Tern. There, the guard has just passed, now — go!'

Tern darted halfway across the cleared area, and then dropped to the ground. The guard didn't see him.

★　★　★

Colonel Lyet found that by swinging his leg from side to side in the strap that supported it, he was able to make a constant banging noise on the wall. The iron pipe that held the strap up went away from the wall and then back with a steady thump, thump, thump. He kept the noise going while he watched the human lump on the ground.

The guard passed the place where the figure lay. The figure rose from the ground, raced to the edge of the fence, and again dropped.

★   ★   ★

Colonel Lyet kept up the steady thump, thump, thump on the wall of his room, but no one came. The guard stolidly continued his marching. Colonel Lyet saw the figure raise an arm. There was something in the intruder's hand that glittered in the beam of the searchlight.

A gun? Lyet wondered. The figure began manipulating the glinting object up against the fence. *Wire cutters!* Lyet kept up the thumping.

'Now, Colonel, you shouldn't be doing that. It keeps the other patients awake.

Didn't anyone give you something to help you sleep?' The night nurse had finally heard the noise.

'Nurse! Come over here and look out the window, quickly.'

'Certainly, Colonel,' the nurse humored him. 'At what?'

The guard had turned, and the interloper was frozen against the fence.

'Look at that man over by the fence.'

'The guard, Colonel?'

'No, not the guard,' Colonel Lyet kept the impatience out of his voice. 'Here — watch the guard as he walks. Now, watch the spot he has just passed.'

As they watched, the small figure pushed up and through the fence.

'Oh! Who's that?' The nurse was startled.

'Someone who shouldn't be there. He's breaking into the area. Is there an MP downstairs?'

'No, but the Officer of the Day has a telephone to the MP squadroom. I'll go and tell him right now.' The nurse turned and scurried from the room.

As Colonel Lyet watched, the figure broke away from the fence and ran into the protective shadow of a truck parked close by. He then raced from the truck to the side of the Motor Pool garage building.

Lights went on in the MP squad room, and figures came running out, some putting on their helmets, some buckling on gun belts as they ran. They headed for the hole in the fence.

The interloper crouched down by the building and waited until the last of the MP's had run past. Then he dashed across the short distance between that building and the next, the Headquarters Company arms room. He pulled something from his back, and placed it on the ground by the building wall. For a moment all motion appeared to cease, and then a blinding explosion shook the fort.

A piece of wood the size of a baseball bat came through the top of Colonel Lyet's window and shattered the glass into small shards which were hurled around the room. One of the shards cut into the pillow beside Colonel Lyet's head, missing him by three inches.

The new radio equipment, the colonel thought. *Again they knew just where to find it. How did they know? That man was blown up in the explosion, they sacrificed him to get the equipment. How the hell did they know it was there?*

★   ★   ★

Phom looked at Captain Quat. 'It's exploded,' he said.

'Yes,' Quat said. 'A beautiful explosion.'

'But Tern didn't have a chance to get away. He must have been blown up with the bomb. What happened?'

Captain Quat shrugged. 'It must have been a faulty timer,' he said.

Phom stared out into the bright light of the burning building. 'A faulty timer — how could that have happened?'

'It's all for the best,' Quat said in a hard voice. 'Someone must have given the alarm. If Tern had gone away and left the bomb there to go off four minutes later, they might have found it and neutralized it before it went off. That was an important target.'

49

'Oh, it's like that, is it?' Phom whispered.

'Shut up and let's get out of here,' Quat said. 'We're making an omelette, and it's necessary to break an occasional egg.'

The two of them faded into the woods.

5

Peter Carthage pushed open the double doors marked 'Administration,' walked over to the receptionist in the room beyond, and murmured 'Death to all who oppose the revolution' in her ear.

Distracted, the girl looked up from her typewriter. 'What's that?' she demanded.

'That's the password,' Peter told her. 'You're supposed to answer, 'Long live our glorious republic,' and push the buzzer so I can go inside.'

'Mister Carthage,' the girl told him severely, adjusting her carefully disarrayed blonde hair, 'you're not funny.'

'No, I suppose not,' Peter admitted sadly. 'I apologize. If you could see it in your heart to forgive me, I would be forever in your debt.'

'I'll think about it,' the girl told him.

'Good,' Peter said. 'While you're thinking, push the buzzer. When I come out, you can tell me what you've decided.'

The receptionist pushed the button on her desk, and Peter went through the door to the corridor beyond. He walked past the closed office doors until he came to one marked 'Thomas Steadman, President.' It opened as he approached, and a tall brunette girl beckoned him in.

'Good morning, Miss Cow,' Peter said cheerfully.

'The receptionist warned me that you were coming,' the girl told him.

'Warned? Is that a fair — '

'Some other time,' Miss Cow said brusquely. 'The Old Man wants to see you right away.'

'I heard. Do you know what it's all about?'

'No, but there's someone in there with him.'

'Well, there's only one way to find out. Would you tell the good doctor I'm here, please?'

Miss Cow announced Peter, and after a few seconds he was admitted to the inner sanctum.

'Ah, Carthage,' Doctor Steadman stood up as Peter entered, 'we've been waiting for you. Ambassador Trimam, this is one of our Expediters, Peter Carthage. Peter, allow me to introduce his Excellency Bhat Eno Trimam, Ambassador to the United States from the kingdom of Bonterre.'

Ambassador Trimam, well dressed in the conservative style of statesmen and undertakers, was quite distinguished-looking. He was a middle-aged man with graying hair and a delicately Asian appearance.

'It's a pleasure to meet you, your Excellency,' said Peter. The ambassador stood up to shake hands. 'The honor is mine,' he answered.

Peter looked questioningly at Doctor Steadman.

'Sit down, Carthage, and let's get down to business,' Steadman said. 'Ambassador Trimam thinks that War, Inc., can provide a useful service for his country.'

'That is so,' the ambassador said to Peter. 'Tell me, what do you know of Bonterre?'

Peter sat in the red leather chair on one side of Steadman's huge desk, and stared at the opposite wall. 'Bonterre,' he said carefully, 'is a monarchy with a population of some fourteen million. It's in an area generally called Indo-China, and was under French control until 1957. In that year the French, er, relinquished control, and handed complete authority back to the king. If I remember correctly, Bonterre was not one of the areas that had extensive guerrilla operations resisting French rule. Principal product: rice; principal exports: rubber and a little oil, with the strong possibility that there might be a lot more oil. Until about fifteen years ago, the main money crop was opium poppy, but the trade has been declared illegal and suppressed successfully.' Peter paused, and then realized that he had run out of facts. 'That's about it,' he admitted.

Ambassador Trimam allowed a fleeting smile to cross his face. 'That's a fair fund of information about a country that most people in this part of the world would be hard pressed to find on a map,' he said. 'However, allow me to extend your knowledge.

'The kingdom of Bonterre,' the ambassador said in a lecture-room voice, 'is one of the oldest on the face of the earth. Our present king, His Royal Highness Min Lhat, whose traditional titles would take five minutes just to quote, can trace his ancestry back into legend. The old religion, which held sway until the country officially converted to Buddhism in the year A.D. 362, held that the royal line was directly descended from the union of the male and female elements of the god that created, among other things, the universe. It was a sort of trinity: male element, female element, and the half-divine, half-human child that became the first king. The symbol of our royal family shows the male and female god-elements combined in the unity that is our king. It was picked up by other countries and religions, and is now known popularly as the yin-yang.

'Over the centuries we have, at various times, been part of the empires of more powerful states. China, Japan and France have all ruled in Bonterre, but always through the person of our hereditary king. When France moved out it was the first time in many centuries that the King was more than a figurehead. He immediately chose to become only a figurehead again.

'King Min Lhat was educated in Europe, and spent two years in the United States during World War Two. He returned to his country with what I can best describe as 'republican' ideas.

'The King caused a group of our leading scholars to draw up a constitution. When they had completed it to his satisfaction, he had it declared irreversible law of the land, and, under its provisions, a parliament was elected. The date chosen was, for symbolic reasons, the fourth of July, 1959. In our study of various constitutional models while planning our own, the scholars were very impressed by the American Constitution and Bill of Rights. Since this date the country of Bonterre has been a constitutional monarchy.'

The ambassador broke off suddenly. 'Am I boring you?' he asked.

'No, not at all. I find it fascinating,' Peter answered honestly.

'Yes,' Steadman added. 'It's an interesting history.'

'I've been accused by my daughter of a

tendency to lecture,' Ambassador Trimam said. 'Before I was appointed ambassador, I was a professor of history and political science. No matter, I was coming to the essential part of the story anyway.

'About a year and a half ago a small group of irregular soldiers — guerrillas — began to create disturbances in the extreme northern part of the country. Over the past eighteen months the guerrillas have increased in number until they're now a serious menace to the population and industry of the country. They actually control some areas of land, and at night they terrorize almost at will. These guerrillas, as far as the government can tell, receive very little popular support, and are using neighboring countries as their sanctuary, base of operations, and source of supply. In the areas of the country they control, they do so through fear and terror.

'Although some few of the officers in our Army were trained in France, the Army seems to be absolutely ineffectual against these guerrillas. They appear out of nowhere, strike at will, and then vanish again.'

'It sounds like a familiar pattern,' Peter commented, 'in some ways altogether too familiar.'

'I was telling the ambassador that we'd seen this mold before,' Steadman said.

'I think you'll find that the jell in this particular mold contains some unusual, even unique, elements,' Ambassador Trimam said.

'In what way?' Doctor Steadman asked.

'There's a — what I guess you would have to call 'third force' — operative in Bonterre.'

'A third force?' Steadman asked. 'What elements make up this third force?'

'Doctor Steadman,' the ambassador leaned forward in his chair, 'didn't you wonder why I came to see you today with no previous warning, no sort of contact by letter or telephone?'

'It had occurred to me,' Steadman admitted, 'but I decided to let you explain. I took the precaution of verifying that you are the ambassador, however.'

Trimam jumped up. 'Not, I hope, by calling the Embassy?' he demanded.

'No, sir.' Steadman shook his head.

'Nothing so crude. I just had a good photograph of you brought around to compare with the person requesting to see me. Reasonable, although not positive, assurance.'

'That's good,' Ambassador Trimam said, relaxing in his chair. 'You see, Doctor Steadman, I'm here without the knowledge of anyone else in my Embassy. I'm not accustomed to doing things behind people's backs, but in this case it seemed essential.'

'This is because of this 'third force' you spoke of?' Peter asked.

'That is so,' the ambassador said. 'This third force is in an unusual position of power in my country. They are violently opposed to the government, and yet many of them are in positions of great importance in that government. They have their representatives in both the legislature and the military. We are aware of who some of these people are, but they have sympathizers and supporters in the government that are unknown to us. If it had become known that I was coming here today my life would have been in danger. These people do not want any sort of outside interference, particularly on the side of the government.'

There was an interruption at this moment. After knocking on the door, Miss Cow entered with a tray holding an electric coffee pot and three cups. 'Sorry to interrupt,' she said, 'but the coffee's ready.'

'Thank you, Cow,' Doctor Steadman said. 'Just put the tray on the side of the desk, and we'll help ourselves.' Miss Cow nodded, put the tray down, and retreated through the door.

Steadman poured the coffee, and then started hunting through his desk for the small pair of silver tongs that he always used with the lump sugar. He reminded Peter of a fussy aunt that he used to visit on Sunday afternoons as a small boy in Ohio.

'Ah,' Steadman said, fishing the tongs out of a side drawer, 'here they are. Please continue with your explanation, Ambassador Trimam. One lump or two?'

Peter sipped his coffee. 'Did I understand you to say that you came here without the knowledge of anyone else in your government?'

'Not quite, Mister Carthage. I came here with the knowledge and at the express wish of my King.'

'Perhaps you'd better explain the situation to us more fully,' Doctor Steadman suggested.

'Yes, I think so. The third force that I speak of can best be described in the terms of your country as being of the far right,' Ambassador Trimam said. 'It is made up of the great landowners, the rubber and oil interests, and some of the high-ranking Army officers. Not all the people in these categories, by any means, but a good number of them.'

'What interest do these people have in seeing the guerrillas win?' Doctor Steadman asked. 'Most guerrilla movements favor a reform program that would break up large holdings and nationalize important industries. I should think that these 'rightists' would be among the most strongly opposed to the guerrillas.'

'Yes,' Trimam said. 'The logic of the situation would seem to indicate that.

61

Unfortunately Bonterre's new democratic government is in the process of enacting laws that would eventually do that very thing anyway. These people think that it's more important that Bonterre's attempt at parliamentary government fail than that the guerrilla force is immediately defeated. We even have reason to believe that they are actively aiding the guerrilla forces. Their logic is that if the guerrillas keep up their activity, the people will lose faith in their government. If the government falls, they would be the natural ones to step into the power vacuum; and then they could proceed to clean up the guerrillas on their own.

'We believe that these rightists are waiting for the peasant population to become completely disenchanted with the government's inability to protect them from guerrillas. The rightists will then try to seize power in a coup d'etat. They think the time when this will be possible is coming fairly soon if things keep up as they are now. And the sad thing is that they're probably right.

'They feel that, once they've taken

power, they'll be able to stop the guerrillas themselves in short order. In that, they're probably wrong. If they take power and eliminate the parliamentary land control and reform measures and other popular legislation as they plan to do, I'm afraid they'll find that the guerrilla force suddenly has strong popular support.'

'I see what you mean,' Peter said. 'People of that sort are seldom able to see beyond the ends of their noses.'

'That's true, Mister Carthage, but these people have long and sensitive noses, and they poke them all about. They're trying to eliminate the Prime Minister because he's an honest and capable man. They're trying to eliminate me because I'm the King's first cousin, and he has confidence in me. They've even tried to kidnap my daughter because the King is fond of her, and they're not above using any sort of influence at hand. They recently stopped all attempts of this nature, and I'm afraid that what this means is that plans for some major move are being made, and they don't want to take any chances until they're ready to strike.'

'Why these strong attempts to influence a king that you describe as only a figurehead?' Peter asked.

'By law Min Lhat has very restricted power, but by custom he's the country's absolute monarch. The law is only seven years old, while the custom is over two thousand years old. Two-thousand-year-old customs die very slowly.'

'I see,' Doctor Steadman said. 'I've got two further questions for you, Ambassador Trimam. The first, what would you expect War, Inc., to do: and the second, what authority would we be given to do what's expected?'

'Yes,' Trimam said, staring at the back of his hands. 'I'll answer you very simply. To the first question, we would have you teach our armed forces how to cope with these guerrillas. To the second question, the ministerial order authorizing your assistance to our Army would be cancelable only by Royal veto, which, under the constitution can only be applied when it is suggested to the King by the Prime Minister. Practically speaking, you'll have as much freedom of action as the guerrillas themselves will allow.'

'What about these right-wing people?' Peter asked.

'They'll probably try to stop or delay you, but we'll do our best to keep them off your back. That's a government problem.' Trimam twisted his hands together and looked unhappy.

'Supposing they are, as you think, aiding the guerrillas?' Peter asked.

'Just find proof of that,' Trimam said, 'and they'll cease to be any sort of problem at all. That would give us the lever we need to get rid of them.'

Doctor Steadman leaned back in his chair. 'What do you think, Peter?' he asked.

'About what, sir?'

'Assuming we take the job, would you like to head our training team in Bonterre?'

'I would like very much to do so,' Peter answered.

'That's what I thought. You've been

chafing at the bit for some time now. I don't think you're overly fond of office work. I'm afraid you'll find there's a good bit of paperwork involved in heading a training team, but try not to let it get you down.'

Peter smiled. 'I'll do my best, sir.'

Doctor Steadman turned to the ambassador. 'There's one thing that must be clearly understood,' he said. 'War, Inc., will train your troops, act as advisors and coordinators and help with new equipment; however, we are not a fighting force. Our men are under specific instructions not to get directly involved.'

'I understand,' Ambassador Trimam said, 'but how are you going to convince the guerrillas?'

'That'll be our problem,' Steadman said. 'With sufficient provocation, my men have been known to ignore those instructions. Peter, how long would it take you to assemble a group and get it ready to leave for Bonterre?'

'One week, sir.'

'Fine. I'll let you know what's required as soon as all the details are worked out.'

'Very good,' Peter said.

'All right,' Steadman told him, 'get to it. The ambassador and I have money to discuss.'

6

As the big jet transport screamed across the Pacific, Peter Carthage sat at a table in the forward lounge with the five section heads who made up the joint command of War, Inc.'s Bonterre force. Some of the men he had known for years, two were recent additions to the staff of War, Inc. All were highly trained specialists in their fields. Tony Ryan, who headed Plans, was an expert in the field of anti-guerrilla warfare. Eric Jurgens, the husky ex-captain of the Swedish Army, in charge of Training and Weapons, knew how to use any weapon from a howitzer to the chopping edge of his hand with lethal skill. Professor Perlemutter, Propaganda and Civil Affairs, a stout, happy man with an uncontrollable mop of hair, combined an expertise in his field with a passion for mathematics. Bob Alvin, in charge of the Mark IX portable field computer, was reputed to be able to make his machine talk, and had actually once worked out a program that had the computer play 'Dixie' on its whirring bank of tapes. John Wander, Electronics and Communications Systems expert, a mild-looking chess fiend who smoked a mixture that smelled like rubber and horsehair from a vast collection of pipes, had written a widely used textbook on the military use of field communications systems.

The plane was divided into two sections: front compartment for the personnel of the Bonterre mission, rear compartment for the various items of equipment the section heads absolutely refused to travel without. Everything from the three table-sized consoles that made up the Mark IX computer to two racks of submachine guns and a case of ammunition for the men in Jurgens' section was stowed in the aft compartment.

'Before we left,' Peter told the section heads, 'I drew up a timetable of what was supposed to happen when.' Jurgens laughed, a hearty bellowing sound. 'Of course, that explains the confusion.'

'It says on my timetable,' Peter continued, manfully ignoring the interruption, 'that

I'm supposed to give you all a final briefing before we land. Unfortunately, I can't think of anything to say that hasn't been said several times already.'

Jurgens started clapping, and the other men joined in. Bob Alvin thumped on the table and exclaimed 'Hear, hear!' in a loud voice.

'I had thought of an acceptable substitute for that speech,' Peter told them, 'but if this is the sort of thing I'm going to have to put up with for the next few months, we can just forget the whole thing.'

'He's sulking,' Jurgens said. 'We have a group leader that sulks.'

'Worse than that,' Peter told him, 'I'm going to go off in a corner and cry into my bottle of Scotch.'

'Into your what?' Tony Ryan asked.

'Bottle of Scotch. Into my bottle of Glenfiddich twenty-year-old Scotch. I brought it along to take the place of a final briefing, but you disrespectful clowns will just have to do without.'

'Oh, sir,' Ryan said. 'Respectfully speaking, oh, sir. Couldn't we have that final briefing, oh, sir?'

Peter took the bottle from his briefcase and set it on the table. 'See if you can find some glasses while I open it,' he directed Ryan. Ryan left the lounge, and Peter attacked the seal on the bottle with his penknife.

In a minute Ryan returned and distributed paper cups around the table. 'Best I could do,' he commented. 'Sorry about that.'

Peter poured the Scotch around and raised his cup. 'To crime?' he suggested.

'I disapprove in principle,' Professor Perlemutter said. 'Could someone suggest a better toast?'

'Confusion to our enemies,' Tony Ryan offered.

'That toast,' Perlemutter told the group, 'was first used by Charles the First of England, and look what happened to him.'

'You're a hard man to please,' Peter told the Professor. 'Drink your Scotch.'

'An excellent suggestion.' Perlemutter neatly drained his cup, and then pulled a large handkerchief from his pocket and patted his lips.

The door to the pilot's cabin opened,

and the copilot came into the lounge. 'We have a rather unusual problem,' he told the group.

Professor Perlemutter gestured with the handkerchief. 'Speak,' he said.

'We can't land,' the copilot said. Loosing this bombshell, he sat down.

'Mechanical trouble?' Peter asked.

'No.' The copilot looked at the men facing him around the table. 'I'm sorry, I shouldn't have put it that way. What I meant was we can't land at the Bonterre airport. We've just been in touch with them by radio and they claim they have no knowledge of the flight, and can't permit us to land.'

'It's started,' Peter said.

'What does that mean?' John Wander asked.

'I'm not sure, but some sort of trouble. Jurgens, get your men ready.'

'Fighting?' Jurgens asked.

'I hope not, but you'd better break out the submachine guns.'

Jurgens poured himself another drink, gulped it down, and then hurriedly left the lounge.

'Listen,' Peter said to the copilot. 'We haven't enough fuel left to go anywhere else. Understand?'

'We've enough fuel to make any of three other — '

'You don't understand,' Peter interrupted. 'We don't have enough fuel to make any other airport safely. You're going to have to make an emergency landing.'

'I get it,' the copilot smiled, 'I'll see what the pilot says, but I think he'll go along with it. They'll have to let us land if we broadcast a mayday. But, then what?'

'Let me worry about that. And, believe me, I will. Tell me what the airport says after you speak to them this time.'

'Will do,' the copilot said, getting up and giving Peter a mocking salute. 'It's not my plane.' He went back into the pilot's cabin, closing the door behind him.

Peter swiveled in his chair to stare out the window. The plane was immersed in white clouds like a fly caught in cotton candy. Little wisps of cloud tugged briefly at the wing as the plane cut through.

Peter was trying to figure out what must be happening in the airport below them. He knew that the ambassador had notified the King and the Prime Minister that War, Inc.'s advance group was coming. The Bonterre airport authorities had been informed of the expected time of arrival of the chartered jet at the same time as the flight plan was filed at Kennedy International in New York. There was no reason to assume the wave-off was a mistake. Someone who knew who was aboard the plane obviously didn't want them to land. Landing at another airport would only delay them a few days at most, so whoever was behind it was just stalling for time. Time to do what? Peter wondered.

The question was, how much was their unknown adversary willing to do to prevent them from landing? Also, did he know that the advance group contained fifteen armed men — Jurgens' squad leaders — or did he think he had only a group of peaceful theoreticians to deal with?

'All set,' Jurgens announced, coming back into the lounge. 'What are you staring at?'

'The face of the unknown,' Peter answered.

'What does it look like?' Professor

Perlemutter demanded from his corner of the lounge.

'I don't know.' Peter turned to face them. 'But I think we're equipped to handle it. It's always good to remember when you're dealing with an unknown force, that they probably know as little about you as you know about them.'

'Philosophy class dismissed,' John Wander said, knocking his pipe against the edge of the seat. 'Field exercises on the Categorical Imperative will commence immediately upon landing the classroom.'

The copilot came back into the lounge. 'We're landing to refuel,' he told Peter, 'with their grudging permission. But we're not to disembark or allow any of the passengers to.'

'Did they give any reason for their lack of hospitality?' Jurgens asked.

'They muttered something about 'political unrest,' but it was a bit vague.'

'I'll bet,' Peter said.

'What's the word, Colonel Carthage?'

'Don't call me 'colonel,'' Peter groused. 'This uniform's is purely for effect.'

'It has an effect on me,' the copilot told

him, 'after six years in the Air Force, whenever I see that eagle on someone's shoulders the saluting reflex takes over.'

'That's why we wear them,' Peter explained. 'Any soldier will listen twice as hard to an instructor who outranks him as he will to a civilian. How far out are we?'

'About ten minutes,' the copilot told him.

'Have you anything like a map of the airport?'

'I've got something very much like a map of the airport. Wait a second, I'll get it.' He disappeared into the pilot's cabin.

'I've issued thirty rounds of ammunition to each man,' Jurgens announced in a bloodthirsty voice.

'Personnel of War, Inc., are at all times to remember that their function is purely advisory,' Professor Perlemutter announced. 'They are to avoid operational combat missions to the best of their ability.'

'What's that?' Jurgens asked.

'Oh, just a quote from our Operations Procedure Manual.'

'We're here as instructors, right?'

Jurgens demanded. 'Well, if they watch us, they'll learn something.' He turned and left the lounge.

'Here's the map,' the copilot called. He unfolded the square of silk and spread it on the table. 'It's the airline chart of the Bonterre area. There,' he said pointing, 'is the airport. We come down on runway two-A, which is this one.'

'And then what?' Peter asked.

'And then we taxi over to this area here, where they'll refuel us.'

'This is the operations building over here?' Peter asked, pointing at another area.

The copilot nodded. 'Operations area, control tower and administration building.'

'Very good,' Peter said studying the map thoughtfully, 'thank you. Please tell me right before you start the landing approach.' He got up and went back to talk to Jurgens and the fifteen squad leaders.

★ ★ ★

Thin Bwat, administrator of the Bonterre International Airport, watched the blip on the radar scope with a certain amount of trepidation. 'You're sure they understood the instructions?' he asked the Aircraft Controller for the third time.

'Yes, sir,' the controller said patiently. 'I had their copilot repeat the instructions back to me.'

'They're to taxi right over to the refueling area?'

'That's what I told them.'

'And no one's to get off the plane at all?'

'Yes, sir.'

'How soon can we get them out of here?'

'Within an hour, sir, for sure.'

'Good.' Thin turned his troubled face back to the radar scope. 'I still wish we didn't have to let them land. I'm going to get in trouble if anything goes wrong.'

'We couldn't very well turn down a request for an emergency landing, sir. If it ever became known that we'd done that, we'd be a ghost airport inside of a week. No major airline would ever land here again.'

'Yes, yes. I know all that. But it's a trick. It must be a trick. I don't know what they expect to gain. I'll make sure that nobody gets off that plane.' He clenched his fist and pounded it against the table. 'If anything goes wrong,' he told the controller, 'you'll be permitted to share the blame.'

'Craft is on final approach path now, sir,' the man at the radar board called. Bwat jumped up and hurried out of the room.

★   ★   ★

'I don't suppose we'll get a ramp pulled up to the door,' Peter told Jurgens. 'You'll have to use the emergency rope ladder.'

Jurgens snorted. 'What is it to the ground? About twelve feet? Don't worry about it, we'll jump out — it's faster.'

'The stuff,' Peter said reverently, 'of which heroes are made.' He went forward to watch the landing.

Almost hesitantly the silver jet touched down at the edge of runway two-A. Large flaps in the wing swung down, and the

79

engines roared in a braking action, slowing the big craft down to taxiing speed. As the plane reached the end of the runway, and turned onto the taxiway leading to the refueling area, four gold and blue airport jeeps pulled away from the terminal building and raced toward the slowing craft.

The jet reached the spot it had been directed to, and swung gently around until it faced the oncoming jeeps. The jeeps pulled up, quartering the plane: one in front, one behind, and one on each side. Each jeep carried four men in Airport Police uniforms. At a signal three men got out of each jeep and spread themselves around the plane, holding their submachine guns at port, and doing their best to look fierce.

'Is there enough room between the two jeeps?' Peter asked the pilot.

'I'll manage.'

'Then let's get the show on the road.'

The pilot adjusted the fuel mixture. 'Brace yourself,' he told Peter.

Peter wedged himself between the navigator's seat and the wall of the crowded compartment. 'Go,' he said.

Thick clouds of oily black smoke poured from the engines of the plane. It wheeled slightly to the left to avoid the jeep in front of it, and then blasted down the field like a startled ostrich. The Airport Police, to a man, dropped their guns and doubled over, holding their ears.

'A full-on jet engine is pretty noisy, if you happen to be standing right behind it,' the pilot commented, as the cops disappeared behind the wall of smoke. 'Well above the pain threshold, I believe.'

Within thirty seconds the plane had crossed the field and braked to a stop in front of the administration building. The plane's door swung open, and armed men in battle dress dropped to the ground two-by-two. Jurgens, in the lead, quickly fanned the men out and directed them into position. Stationing two men at each of the three doors leading onto the field, he took the rest of his men into the building and up the main stairs to the control room. The three native policemen left in the building were too bewildered to even draw their pistols, and were disarmed without incident.

The eight men in the control room froze when Jurgens and his men burst in.

'Who's in charge here?' Jurgens barked in French.

A stout Bonterrian in a dark brown suit with wide lapels broke out of his trance. 'What's the meaning of this?' he squeaked.

'My question exactly,' Jurgens demanded.

By this time the gold and blue police jeeps had reached the plane. The machine-gun-carrying policemen jumped out and, obviously lacking both orders and initiative, clustered in a circle behind their vehicles and pointed their weapons around them nervously.

A rope ladder was dropped from the open door of the plane and, slowly and with dignity, Peter Carthage climbed down onto the soil — or at any rate the concrete — of Bonterre. The police made no attempt to stop him as he walked from the plane to the building. The two squad leaders at the door Peter entered snapped to attention and saluted as he passed. One of them winked. Returning the salute and the wink, Peter muttered, 'Keep it cool, boys. We've got them running around in circles.' He walked up the stairs to the control room.

'That's the boss,' Jurgens told Peter as he entered the room. 'His name's Thin Bwat.'

Peter looked at the fat man facing him. His father must have had a sense of humor, he thought. 'Mister Bwat. I am Colonel Carthage, head of the War Inc., advisory group to the Bonterre Army.'

Bwat extended his hand with a jerky motion, and waited for it to be shaken. Peter regarded the outstretched limb without enthusiasm and didn't reach for it. 'May I ask what's going on here?'

Bwat withdrew his hand. 'Going on . . . ' he started. 'I, er, I'm not sure . . . ' he trailed off.

'Did you give the order for us not to land?'

'Well,' Bwat said. He looked away from Peter, and found that he was staring at Jurgens, who shifted his machine gun around so that the muzzle pointed at Bwat. He looked back at Peter. 'We had no notification . . . ' he began.

'If I look in your logbook, I won't find any notification of the planned arrival of this flight?' Peter asked.

For the life of him, Bwat couldn't remember whether the offensive document had been removed from the record. 'There may have been some mistake,' he said in a low voice.

'What's that? Speak up!'

'I said, there may have been some mistake. An oversight of some sort. If you, er, people actually do have landing papers on record here, I'm sure we can straighten everything out.'

'Why don't you take a look?' Peter suggested in a reasonable voice.

'Yes,' Jurgens put in with a wave of his gun, 'I think you'll find the papers if you look.'

'Yes,' Thin Bwat said, 'of course. I'll look right now.' He started leafing through some loose leaf notebooks on the big desk.

There was the sound of a brief scurry at the door, and a Bonterre Army colonel strode into the room. 'What's going on here?' he demanded.

Jurgens muttered, 'This sounds like a repeat,' and swung his weapon around to cover the colonel.

'Who are you?' Peter asked.

'Francis Lyet, Colonel, Royal Army of Bonterre. And who the hell are you?'

'Peter Carthage, Group Commander, War, Incorporated's Bonterre Mission.'

'You're the people I was sent down here to meet,' the colonel said. 'What the hell's going on around here? It looks like your people have taken over the airport.'

'That's about it, Colonel,' Peter told him. 'It seemed to be the only way we could get off the plane.'

'You'll have to explain that,' Colonel Lyet said.

'Talk to the thin man here.' Jurgens used his gun as a pointer to indicate Bwat, who was trying hard to fade into the metalwork.

'Yes?' the colonel asked, staring at Bwat.

'Thin Bwat, your excellency,' Bwat explained.

'I'm not anybody's excellency,' Colonel

Lyet said angrily. 'Now, what's happening around here?'

'I, er, couldn't find any authority for these people to land, your ex — Colonel, so I was forced to wave their plane off. Then they requested emergency permission to land for refueling, which I, of course, couldn't refuse,' Bwat said, wishing he had. 'I put out a, er, routine guard which they circumvented.'

'When did we start the policy of waving planes — any planes — away from the airport?' Colonel Lyet asked softly, advancing toward Bwat.

'I, er, may have made a mistake,' Bwat admitted.

'That's possible,' Lyet told him. 'You may even have lost a job. There's even a chance criminal charges will be brought up against you. I'm going to see that this incident has a full investigation.' Colonel Lyet turned to Peter. 'If you'll relinquish control of the airport, I have transportation for you and your men outside. We were expecting you, although I must apologize for the welcome.'

'Certainly, Colonel,' Peter said. He told

Jurgens to assemble the men.

'I must admit,' Colonel Lyet told Peter as they walked toward the waiting car, 'that I was hostile to the idea of a group coming here to train us, but it certainly seems as if you men know what you're doing.'

7

'I have to go?' Jurgens asked. 'I mean, can't you say I broke a leg, or something?'

'Sorry about that,' Peter said, adjusting his dress uniform with the Advisor patch on the shoulder. 'After all, these are the people we're going to have to work with, so we might as well get to know them as soon as possible.'

'I know, but a goddam reception. I hate goddam receptions. Walking around all evening sipping cocktails and eating crackers, smiling and answering stupid questions.'

Peter slapped Jurgens on his massive back. 'Cheer up, Eric. Think of it as a part of your job.'

'Ya, a part of my job it is. We should get boring-duty pay.'

Professor Perlemutter came into the room struggling with the wide red sash around his dress suit. 'Very nice hotel rooms they've given us,' he commented.

'Are you about ready?'

'What's that medal you're wearing on the sash?' Peter asked him.

Perlemutter looked down at the ornate piece of gold resting on his large belly with interest. 'I'm not sure,' he said.

'You don't know?' Jurgens boomed.

'They told me when I bought it,' Perlemutter explained, 'but I've forgotten.'

'You bought it?' Peter asked.

'Of course, of course. I wear it only to impress the natives.'

Jurgens started to laugh. 'That stomach should impress them quite enough. It impresses me.'

Professor Perlemutter slapped at his middle. 'It's taken me a good many years to acquire,' he said with satisfaction. 'Americans all try to be skinny, I can't understand it. In my country a skinny man is considered either dishonest or incapable.'

'You must be one of the world's most honest men,' Jurgens told him.

'What are you going to say if someone asks what the medal is for?' Peter asked.

'My dear boy,' Perlemutter reassured him. 'No one would be so impolite as to do that.'

'You're probably right,' Peter admitted. 'Well, let's get some road under this show.'

The chauffeured limousine drove Peter and his five section heads through Bonterre City. Their driver kept up a running commentary of the points of interest in bad French.

'The, what you would call, district of finance we pass through now,' he told them at one point. 'Four banks.' They looked properly impressed.

'The district of nightclub amusements,' the driver said, turning a corner onto a brightly lit street.

'And I thought Times Square was garish,' Tony Ryan said.

'The invention of the neon tube has done a lot to raise the standard of living in underprivileged countries,' Professor Perlemutter explained.

'Thousands of watts of electrical power for lighting, and they can't even pave the streets,' said John Wander.

'Tried paving streets better,' the driver said, 'but rainy season washes away paving.' He turned another corner. 'Is palace,' he said.

In front of them an imposing building rested behind iron gates. It looked like a cross between a cathedral and a hall of justice, and would have been a 'Point of Interest' in any guidebook.

'Wow,' Tony Ryan said, 'quite a change.'

'Is builded by French,' the driver explained. He stopped at one of the gates long enough for a guard to identify the official car, and then entered the driveway. Brilliant floodlights covered every section of the grounds.

'It's lit up like a centennial exposition,' Bob Alvin commented in English.

'Please?' the driver asked in French. The phrase was translated for him. 'Is recent,' he explained. 'Is lights put in only after terrorist attacks and bombs happen in city.'

The car pulled up to the front door, and the group got out. A uniformed major-domo escorted them down the marble and mirror hallway. At the end of the hall a pair of gilt double doors stood open with a guard at either side. The guards, Peter noticed, were in some sort of traditional court dress, with baggy white pants and bright red sashes, but they carried modern rifles polished to an almost impossible gloss.

'The household troops,' Jurgens muttered.

A tuxedo with white tie came out to greet them. 'Ah, Mister Carthage, it's good to see you again.'

'Ambassador Trimam. I didn't know you were here.'

'I arrived two days ago. It's my honor to be able to greet you.'

'Thank you, sir. Allow me to present the section leaders of our mission.' Peter introduced them to Trimam, who shook hands formally with each of them.

'Let me explain to you the protocol for this evening,' Trimam said, leading the group into the ballroom. 'You're not to be formally presented to the King until tomorrow, but you'll meet him here later. There'll be no formality here tonight, that will be reserved for tomorrow. Think of this as a large cocktail party.'

'Large indeed,' Professor Perlemutter said, looking around the huge room. 'There must be six hundred people in here.'

'Closer to a thousand,' Ambassador Trimam told him, 'and you'll be introduced to most of them. Everyone in Bonterre that is of the least importance, or thinks he is, is in this room: government officials, foreign embassy staffs down to the secretaries, merchants, shopkeepers, plantation owners, planters, miners and both the native and the leftover French aristocracy.'

'I didn't realize we were that important,' Peter said.

'So? Well, remember that fully half of the people would be very happy to see your mission fail.'

'Cheerful,' Peter said.

'Into the valley of death,' Jurgens said. He put on a smile, and marched forward.

Peter followed Trimam into the crowd, smiling, shaking hands and repeating names which he promptly forgot. Letting the others get slightly ahead of him, he managed to get out of the crush sufficiently to snare a passing waiter carrying a tray of drinks. He examined the drinks on the tray. 'Martini?' he asked, pointing to a colorless liquid in a stemmed glass.

The waiter nodded his head emphatically.

'Good,' Peter said, taking the glass. 'Gin or vodka?'

Again the waiter nodded his head emphatically.

'I see,' Peter said. 'It's definitely either gin or vodka. You're a big help.'

The waiter nodded again.

'You speak fluent English, of course?' Peter asked.

The waiter kept nodding.

'Parlez-vous français?'

The waiter bowed from the waist, and looked nervous.

'You must think I'm picking on you,' Peter continued in French. 'Not so. I'm quite aware that I don't speak your language any better than you speak mine. It's not your fault.' He smiled at the waiter and raised the drink to his lips. The waiter went away. Peter sipped the drink and then spat back into the glass. The inside of his mouth felt like someone had just used a blowtorch on it. '*Merde!*'

'That's not very nice, Colonel,' a very feminine voice purred at him in French.

Peter turned. The woman speaking was tall, blonde, and had that solid beauty that is traditionally French. Her full lips were arranged in a pout, but her eyes twinkled.

'I apologize for my bad manners, mademoiselle.'

'It's madame.' She extended a gloved hand. 'Madame DuMarte.'

'A pleasure.'

'I hope so,' she smiled. 'You are Colonel Carthage?'

'My fame seems to have preceded me,' Peter grinned. 'Am I going to have the honor of seeing you and your husband during my stay in Bonterre?'

'I hope to see a lot of you,' Madame DuMarte said. She pursed her lips. 'I'm a widow.'

'Flirting again, Annette?' a clipped voice demanded.

'Ah, Richard.' Madame DuMarte plunged into the milling crowd and returned with a close-cropped man in tow. 'Colonel, may I present Richard Logan — Richard, Colonel Carthage. Richard is also an American.'

'It's a pleasure to meet you,' Peter said politely. 'Didn't expect to meet many Americans here.'

'One isn't many, is it?' Logan asked. 'What are you a colonel in?'

Peter surveyed the unpleasant young man from his close-cropped hair to his well-shined shoes. 'It's an equivalency rank,' Peter said. 'What do you do here in Bonterre?'

'I represent things.'

'Things?'

'American companies and business interests.'

'I see,' Peter said. 'You were obviously picked for your manners.'

'Now, now,' Madame DuMarte said. 'It seems to be a case of instant dislike. That's ridiculous, you two should be friends. I hope to see you soon, Colonel Carthage.'

'I hope so too,' Peter called, as she steered Logan across the room. He rejoined the rest of his group, who were clustered about Ambassador Trimam as though for protection.

'Ambassador,' Peter called. 'What sort of local poison have I picked up in this glass?'

'Let's see it,' Trimam said. Peter handed it over. Trimam swirled the liquid around in the glass, and then tasted it. 'Ah!' he said. 'Yes. Gart rhandi, a jovial, hearty, but rather powerful beverage. It's quite popular around here.'

'It'll take some getting used to,' Peter said, 'but I might as well start now.' He took the glass back.

'Say,' Jurgens said, 'where'd you get the drink?'

'One of the waiters,' Peter told him, 'but it's kind of strong.'

'That'll be a relief.' Jurgens headed off toward the nearest waiter.

★ ★ ★

'It's about time,' Trimam said a few minutes later.

'For what?'

'To meet the King. He wants a chance

to talk to you before he comes into the main ballroom, it'll be less hectic.'

'Fine,' Peter said. 'Where is he?'

'If you'll retrieve your compatriot, I'll take you.'

Peter called Jurgens back, and the group filed out of the ballroom and up the staircase.

'In here,' Trimam said, stopping before an ornate door. He knocked.

'Enter.'

Trimam opened the door. 'Your Majesty, allow me to present the personnel of the War, Incorporated, mission.'

'Ah, yes. That wonderful group who are going to save my country from ruin, for a fee. Come in, gentlemen, come in; I've been waiting to meet you. Ignore my sarcasm and, instead, accept my gratitude at your being here at all.'

It was a small room, not overly furnished. King Min Lhat, in a severely tailored black dress coat, was sitting behind a heavy oak desk littered with papers. At the side of the desk a very beautiful girl in a deep red evening dress was struggling with a large notebook.

'My private office,' King Min told them, 'and Miss Marya Trimam, my private secretary, my niece, and daughter of Ambassador Trimam. Since he's my first cousin, I suppose, actually, Marya's my second cousin.'

'First cousin once removed, I believe, Your Majesty,' Marya told him.

'Ah,' said the king.

The ambassador introduced them to King Min one at a time, starting with Peter.

'Pull up chairs, gentlemen. I'd like to speak to you briefly before we go downstairs. Marya, you may leave.'

'Uncle!' the girl pouted.

'Marya, you may stay.' The King shrugged. 'Here I am, gentlemen, titular head of Bonterre, helpless at the hands of an eighteen-year-old girl.'

'Most men are helpless at the hands of such a beautiful woman,' said Peter. Marya favored him with a breathtaking smile.

'It is so,' the King agreed. 'And now, gentlemen, I'd like you to give me some idea of your plans and how you intend to proceed.'

'That'd be hard to say,' Peter explained. 'Each case is different, and we'll have to do a study of your problem first. Why don't I have each of my section heads give you a rundown on the techniques and methods he uses?'

The King agreed, and spent the next twenty minutes getting a series of lectures on the theory and practice of anti-guerrilla warfare.

'Thank you all,' he said when the last speech was over. 'If I can be of any assistance to you at any point, please let me know. You people sound like you know what you're talking about, and we'll certainly give it a try. Rest assured that everyone concerned will be directed to cooperate with you completely. I think Trimam's made a good choice. And now, gentlemen, we'd best be going downstairs.'

8

There's a certain sameness about modern hotels, Peter reflected from the comfort of his bed the next morning. From inside a room it would be impossible to tell whether it was New York or Teheran, Bombay or Bonterre. He turned his travel alarm off and tried to go back to sleep.

'Well,' Eric Jurgens observed, throwing open the door to the connecting room, 'breakfast time.'

'Unproven assumption,' Peter growled, pulling up the blanket.

Jurgens pulled the covers off the bed. 'You don't want to set a bad example for the rest of the men, do you?'

'I won't tell them,' Peter said, but he swung his legs over the side of the bed.

'I'll order breakfast — what do you want?'

'See if you can get half a grapefruit to go with my coffee. That'll do me.'

'Come on,' Jurgens said, 'we're not going to be at the hotel much longer, you might just as well take advantage of it.'

'I was trying to,' Peter told him, pulling his bathrobe on, 'but you insisted on waking me up.'

Jurgens pulled the telephone to him and asked for room service. 'Two orders,' he said, 'the first for four scrambled eggs, a double order of ham, croissants, milk and coffee; and the other for half a grapefruit and coffee. Room four-oh-four.' Peter retreated to the bathroom to take a shower. When he came out Jurgens was just wiping up the last of his eggs with the remains of a croissant.

'I've missed breakfast,' Peter said, staring at the disordered tray.

'I salvaged your grapefruit,' Jurgens told him. 'Sit down and have coffee with me.'

'Fine.' Peter sat down and rummaged through the plates to find his grapefruit.

'What's on for today?' Jurgens asked.

'Well, let's see. You take your crew out to start on Fort Alpha today. You've got two weeks to get the fencing and the prefab barracks and classrooms up before the first cycle starts training. A company of Bonterre infantry are going up with you as a permanent party, so figure out the best way to utilize them.'

'Two weeks?' Jurgens commented. 'It'll be tight, but we'll make it.'

'Be careful for the first couple of weeks. The guerrillas seem to have a very good intelligence setup, and it would be a smart propaganda move for them to pull a successful raid on the base while we're still building it.'

'I'll take your advice into consideration.'

'Thanks. That should take care of you, Bob Alvin and John Wander for the next few weeks. Professor Perlemutter is planning to wander off on his own and do whatever it is we pay him for. Tony Ryan's the only problem.'

'What's his hang-up?'

'He wants to find a real live guerrilla to interview. It seems that the best the Army can do for him was captured two weeks ago and has gone stale or something.'

There was a knock on the door.

'Come in,' Peter called. Colonel Lyet entered the room in full battle dress.

'I'm sorry to interrupt your meal, gentlemen,' Lyet said, allowing his voice to show what he thought of soldiers who ate breakfast as late as eight o'clock, 'but we're going to look over a town that was hit by guerrillas last night, and I thought you might be interested in coming along.'

'You were right, Colonel, and I thank you,' Peter told him. 'I'll get Mister Ryan and meet you downstairs.' He strapped on his holstered pistol, picked up his field jacket and headed out of the room.

'Very good,' Colonel Lyet said. 'Be as fast as possible, will you?'

'Sure thing, Colonel. See you tonight, Eric.' He raced down the hall and pounded on Tony Ryan's door. Tony was just finishing breakfast and was ready to go as soon as he gulped down his coffee.

'The name of the village is Sihn Long,' Colonel Lyet told them as they bounced over the dirt road in the lead jeep. 'It seems to have been a hit-and-run raid, with no particular objective. They shot up the police station, blew up a commercial radio and executed the headman.'

'Sounds like a good night's work,' Tony said.

'It's a pattern they've been following

recently. Strike at a town, blow up a few things, murder a few people, then disappear into the night. The only object seems to be to frighten the civilian population.'

'That's probably part of it,' Peter said. 'They're also probably trying to make you spread your forces too thin to be effective against a big strike.'

'Yes,' Lyet admitted, 'there is that. What's the cure?'

'Firepower and mobility,' Ryan told him. 'Be ready to slap instantly at wherever they sting, and slap hard.'

'What's needed,' Peter said, 'is good intelligence and a good communications system. Instead of having small defense units in each town, have powerful units carefully distributed, able to jump when and where needed. If possible, the towns should be encouraged to arm themselves in some sort of home defense setup.'

'So,' Colonel Lyet said. 'I've heard these theories being advanced before, and I'm becoming convinced. But I think we have an additional problem that has to be taken care of if any of this is to work.' The jeep took a bad bounce. 'Slow down a little,' he growled at the driver. 'Sihn Long will still be there if it takes us an extra minute or two.'

'What's this additional problem, Colonel?' Tony asked.

'Let me tell you a story,' Lyet said. 'Three weeks ago we were getting ready to set up a system to allow the villages to notify nearby Army units in case of trouble. The first thing the guerrillas do when they raid a town, of course, is cut the phone lines. Now, what we did was to order four hundred set-frequency radio transceivers to use in a network that would include villages and military units. The radios arrived by plane, were secretly loaded into trucks and delivered to a fort in the interior. That night the building being used to store the radios was blown up in a suicide raid.'

'How'd the guerrillas know the radios were there?' Tony asked.

'That's our problem. They have more than just good intelligence, they seem to be psychic.'

'Who knew of the radios?'

'As few as possible. The cases they

came in were even marked as emergency rations.'

'You've got a problem,' Peter admitted. 'We'll keep it in mind.'

Lyet snorted. 'You do that. Let's see what you miracle men come up with.' Then he added: 'I'm sorry, I shouldn't have said that.'

'If that's your attitude, you've masked it very well up to now,' said Peter. 'Let's make a deal. If you agree not to make up your mind about us until you see what we are and aren't capable of doing, I'll agree to do the same for your army.'

'I think you're being subtle, Mister Carthage. However, I agree.'

'That's fine,' Peter said. The jeep jounced to a stop beside a red brick building, and everyone climbed out. A few seconds later the other three jeeps pulled neatly into line and parked.

'Sihn Long,' Colonel Lyet announced. He gathered his men around him. 'Major Bettle, take your team and start through the village. See how many people you can find that actually saw the raid, and get their stories.'

'Yes, sir. Will do.' The major saluted and trotted off down the street with his eight-man team.

The town, a double row of red brick buildings facing a single badly paved road, sat in the middle of a flat scrub jungle area. The paved road began with the first building and ended abruptly with the last building, like an asphalt bridge between two sections of dirt road. The buildings were uniform in appearance, all two stories high except for a more ornate four-story structure like a division marker in the middle of the row.

Peter and Tony joined the group of majors and captains which had gathered around Colonel Lyet, and were listening to him deliver an on the spot lecture.

'This town,' Lyet was saying, 'was built by French interests some thirty years ago as a factory town for workers in rubber processing. The designs of the buildings were purchased in bulk from an architect in France, where they make a lot more sense. Notice the inverted-V shape of the roofs. Perfect for supporting the tons of snow that might pile up during Bonterre's nonexistent winters. The small windows, which are fine for keeping out the cold.'

The group started off down the street.

The natives, who had first dived into prepared hiding places at the sound of approaching trucks, were starting to come out on the street to observe their Army at work.

'Motor noises these days,' Colonel Lyet explained to Peter and Tony, 'mean either Army or guerrillas. They have a habit of stealing them to use on a raid, and then abandoning them outside of the town.'

'What about civilian vehicles?' Peter asked.

'Very few. There's a bus that comes through here once a day. Almost all goods are transported by bullock-cart. For long distance shipping, there's a train. That is, when the tracks haven't been blown up by our friends of the night.'

Signs of last night's raid were evident all along the street. The pockmarks of bullets scored the brick walls, and many of the store fronts were freshly boarded up. It seemed, as Colonel Lyet remarked, an excess of violence to use against an unarmed town. One of the buildings, the four-story one in the center of town, seemed to have been marked out for special attention. The whole ground floor front had been blown out by explosive charges, and most of the windows on the upper floors were machine-gunned out.

'It's the area headquarters building for the local government,' Colonel Lyet explained, 'the equivalent of a town hall and county seat combined. It's the building the guerrillas dragged the headman out of before they shot him.'

'That's cute,' Ryan said. 'All in the classical tradition of Mao Tse-tung and Al Capone.'

'Al Capone?' Lyet asked.

'An American folk hero,' Peter explained.

One of the captains from Major Bettle's group came out of a building and ran over to Colonel Lyet. A rapid conversation in Sadari, the native language of Bonterre, followed between Lyet and the captain. After a minute the captain saluted and ran back into the building.

'Anything for us?' Peter asked.

'It could be,' the colonel told him. 'It looks like we have established the cause of the raid. The guerrillas are trying to levy a head tax on the town. The villagers refused to pay, and so the guerrillas came in to collect a few heads as a warning.'

'Is this the first time the guerrillas have attempted to tax civilians?' Tony asked.

'I believe so. It looks like the start of a new phase in the war. Bah,' Lyet spat. 'New phase. I still think they're nothing but a bunch of bandits. I hate dignifying their murders by calling it a phase.'

'I know how you feel,' Peter told the colonel.

Tony Ryan had dropped to his knees and was rooting around in the street.

'What are you doing?' Lyet asked.

'Merely my famous imitation of Sherlock Holmes,' Tony told him. 'I have here one of the shells fired by the guerrilla horde in the night-time.' He exhibited a brass rifle shell. 'It would seem,' he continued, looking over the shell, 'to be of 7.65 caliber and of western European manufacture. I would say French.'

'Astounding, Ryan,' Peter said.

'Elementary, my dear Carthage,' Tony said modestly.

A sharp cracking sound split the air, and Peter felt the breeze of something pass his right ear. It was followed immediately by another sound, and one of the majors jerked back like a badly operated marionette and fell to the ground. Almost without thinking about it, the whole group hit the dirt.

'Rifle fire,' Tony breathed.

'Amazing,' Peter said, crawling behind a jeep and cautiously raising his head above the hood.

Another shot rang out, and brick shards splattered from the building.

'I saw the flash,' Peter called out. 'On the roof of that building — the tall one.'

'Let's get 'em,' Tony called. He got to his feet, and he and Peter, closely followed by Colonel Lyet, dashed across the street. Peter flattened up against the wall of the building and carefully approached the entrance. Pulling his Colt .38 Special from the holster, he pointed its six inches of barrel through what was left of the door and peered cautiously around the frame, keeping his head about a foot off the pavement. The inner

112

hallway was clear. With Tony and Colonel Lyet covering him, Peter gingerly made his way down the hall to the staircase. It also was empty.

'Let's go up to the roof,' Tony called.

'You two go on up,' Lyet said. 'I'll be with you as soon as I get my men deployed around the building.'

Guns in hand, Peter and Tony climbed the four flights to the roof. They kicked open the door, and peered out. The roof, unlike those of the two-story buildings around, was flat with a tarred top. There was no one up there.

'I know I saw the flash come from here,' Peter said.

'You're right,' Tony told him. 'Look.' He pointed to the front of the building, where two brass shell casings glinted in the sun.

'Well, well,' Peter said. He walked over to the casings, making a slight popping sound every time he took a step. 'The tar is sticky,' he commented.

'Ah,' Tony said. He crouched down and examined the roof. 'Oh, well. It's not quite sticky enough to take footprints,' he said.

'Pity.' Peter picked up one of the shells. 'What do you know, 7.65.'

'Better than that,' Tony said from the rear of the building, 'here's the rifle.' He waved his prize in the air.

'You've found something, gentlemen?' Colonel Lyet asked, coming out on the roof with two of his majors.

'The sniper seems to have disappeared,' Tony said, 'but he left us a memento.'

'May I see that?' Colonel Lyet asked.

Tony handed him the gun. 'It's a Suomi, made in Finland, with a French spotting scope.'

'I wonder why he left it behind,' Peter mused.

'Look here, Colonel,' one of the majors called, 'here's where he got away.'

They went over to the back of the building, where the major was peering over the ledge. 'What did you find?' Lyet asked.

'A ladder, a rope ladder. Right over here.'

The rope ladder was fastened by two hooks to a projection which ran around the roof, supporting the rain gutter. It dangled down the side of the building, just about reaching the ground.

'Just the right length,' Tony said. 'Two shots, bang bang, drop the ladder off the back and split for the woods. He must be four miles away by now.'

'I wonder,' Peter said.

Peter bent down and examined the two hooks holding the ladder up.

'Do you think you could climb down this thing, Tony?' he asked.

'Is that your problem? Sure, nothing to it. Watch.'

'Wait a second,' Peter said. He pulled the hooks free of the little holes in the ledge, and moved the ladder over a few feet to the right. 'There, now let's see you climb down.'

'Tony Tarzan at your service,' Tony said. He climbed over the balcony and started down the ladder. It swayed from side to side violently as he climbed, but held firm, and he reached the bottom without any trouble.

'Very good,' Peter called. 'Go around the building and come back up the stairs.' He turned to the colonel. 'Is that how it was done?'

'How many ways are there to climb

115

down a rope ladder?' the colonel asked.

'You'll have to find a better way than that,' Peter told him. 'Look.' He jerked the steel hooks loose from where they had worked their way into the ledge. 'Look at the holes.' The two holes had been enlarged and deepened by Tony's weight as he climbed down. They were roughly three times the size of the other set of holes in every dimension.

'Ah, so,' Colonel Lyet said, examining the evidence. 'Our assassin clearly didn't leave the roof by that ladder.'

'Then he must still be in the building,' the major volunteered.

'I was about to finish my exhibition of the great detective by suggesting that we search the building for a man with tar on his shoes,' Peter said, and proceeded to explain his logic.

'Is there anything else to which you would direct our attention?' Tony asked in a respectful manner.

'To the curious incident of the dog in the night-time.'

'What dog?' asked the major.

'It is a reference to that great English

116

detective Mister Sherlock Holmes, is it not?' Colonel Lyet asked. 'I read of his exploits while in Paris.'

'You've got it, Colonel, that's right.'

'Reassuring,' said Lyet. 'Major, have this building searched for a man with traces of tar on his shoes, and bring him to me when he's found.'

The major saluted, did an about face, and raced off down the stairs.

Tony chuckled. 'The hunt is on,' he said, 'and the game — '

'Don't say it,' Peter groaned.

'Shall we go downstairs?' Colonel Lyet suggested. 'Let's see how the interview and search team is doing.'

★　★　★

Twenty minutes later a man in a short-sleeved white shirt and light-color pants, the unofficial dress of the government employee, was hustled out of the building and up to Colonel Lyet by two soldiers. The major in charge of the search came up and saluted smartly. 'We have a suspect, sir.'

'Tar on his shoes?' Lyet asked.

'Yes, sir. Also on his trouser knees.'

'Ah, so,' Lyet said. He examined the telltale black smudges on the neatly pressed pants. 'What have you to say for yourself?' he asked the prisoner.

The man looked up at Lyet expressionlessly and said nothing.

'Why the pot shots at us?' Tony chimed in. The man didn't even look at Tony.

'What's your name?' Lyet asked.

'Sam,' the prisoner replied in a dull voice.

'Sam what?' Peter asked.

'Ding Sam.'

'Let me,' Colonel Lyet said to Peter. 'If you have any questions when I'm done, you'll have your turn.'

Lyet continued the interrogation.

'You work in the building?'

'Yes.'

'What's your job?'

'Post office. Clerk.'

'Did you shoot at us?'

No answer.

'Do you deny shooting at us?'

No answer.

'If you tell us what we ask now, it will

118

save us having to check your fingerprints against those on the rifle.'

'Yes.'

'Yes, what?'

The prisoner stared off into space, as if he had lost any interest in the proceedings. He allowed his incurious gaze to rest on Peter for a second.

'Wait,' Peter said. He stepped forward and examined Ding Sam's eyes closely. It confirmed what he had thought he saw. 'This man's pupils are dilated to the size of dimes. He's hopped up on something.'

Colonel Lyet twisted Sam's head and checked for himself. 'Opium,' he snorted.

'His breath doesn't have the smell. Sen-Sen?' Tony suggested.

'Not opium,' Peter said, 'heroin. Look at his arms.' He pulled Sam's arms straight, palms up, to show the familiar track marks of anyone who regularly takes intravenous injections.

'Indeed,' Colonel Lyet said. 'That's very peculiar. While opium addiction is common in parts of Bonterre, the use of heroin is just about unknown. Your discovery presents more problems than it solves.'

'What do we do with him?' Tony asked.

'I suggest the prison ward of a hospital,' Peter said. 'Put him in one of the trucks and guard him until we get back.'

Lyet directed the major. The prisoner was taken away. 'I'll question him further tonight when the drug's worn off. He should be much more amenable to supplying answers when he's been deprived of access to the fantasy world he's in now.'

'Let me know what he says,' Peter asked, 'I'm very curious to find out who wants us dead.'

'You think the shots were aimed at you?'

'Probably. Either at us or at you. That was a special stakeout, and whoever set it had big game in mind.'

They climbed back into the jeep, and the convoy started back to Bonterre.

*　*　*

That night, as Peter was going over the preliminary ground plans for Fort Alpha with Jurgens, he received a phone call.

'Colonel Lyet here. I thought you'd

want to know. I just went over to question Ding Sam. I found him dead in his cell.'

'Dead?'

'Strangled. No more than ten minutes before I got there. We're starting investigations, but I have a feeling that we won't find very much. Something else that might interest you: Thin Bwat, the airport administrator who gave you all the trouble, has disappeared.'

'Well. It sounds like a well-organized group.'

'The rightists pulled that one. Our dead assassin could have been either a rightist or a guerrilla. Both sides seem to have a hell of a better intelligence setup than we do.'

'We'll have to do something about that. Thank you for calling, Colonel.' Peter hung up.

'Trouble?' Jurgens asked.

'The mind boggles,' Peter told him, 'but we'll work it out.'

9

Fort Alpha rose in an area on the outskirts of the capital. Its front gate was on the main road out of the city, while the back fence pressed hard against the jungle. It already had a permanent look, although less than three weeks had gone by since Eric Jurgens had first started to carve it out of the jungle. The barracks were semi-prefabricated wooden frame structures, and looked like barracks have looked since the time of Frederick the Great. The parade grounds were sparse and muddy, as is the inevitable prerogative of parade grounds everywhere.

The sign over the gate was new. FORT ALPHA, in a semicircle of black letters, framed the green and gold insignia of the Bonterre Special Forces. Newly adopted, a green palm tree with a golden lightning bolt superimposed, it would be the device of the graduates of War, Inc.'s antiguerrilla training center.

'This is it,' Jurgens said proudly, as their jeep pulled up to the main gate. An alert-looking MP checked their passes, and then waved them through the gate.

'The first class of officers and men arrived this morning,' Jurgens told Peter. 'They're going through processing now.'

'Where are the instructors' barracks?' Peter asked.

'That one over there,' Jurgens said, pointing to one building in a row of freshly painted identical structures.

Peter said, 'Before I drop off my bags, why don't you give me the guided tour of the post?'

'Certainly,' Jurgens told him, skidding the jeep around a corner. 'On your right, the scenic quartermaster building, where you will observe a line of tourists waiting to pay their shilling for the guided tour.' He indicated a building where a file of Bonterre Army officers were entering one door empty handed and leaving through another door laden with the equipment they'd need for the two-month training program.

'Fort Alpha — named after the Duke, I

123

believe?' asked Peter.

'His father,' Jurgens assured him. 'Next in the line is the Post Arms Room, where the heavy weapons are kept.'

'The arquebuses.'

'And battering rams. This building here, which you will notice is a bit separated from the rest, houses our Mister Alvin with his crew of geniuses and their giant adding machine.'

'Why is it separated from the rest?' Peter asked.

'Bad planning. Now we come to an open space, which you will notice is designated in your guidebook as 'the clearing.' In the center of the clearing you will observe a tower, which is poetically named 'the tower in the clearing,' after the man who erected it. It may seem a bit small to you . . . '

Peter dutifully examined the thirty-foot transmitting tower and the network of guyed wires holding it up. 'It's young yet. With proper care, it'll grow quite nicely.'

'I hope so,' Jurgens said; 'one can never tell in a climate like this.'

Jurgens continued the tour and the

banter until they reached the rear area of the fort. 'This is it,' he said. 'Jungle from here out. Easy access to a jungle area for training was one reason we picked this site.'

'It also gives the guerrillas perfect cover to launch an attack on the fort from, but I suppose you've thought of that.'

'We have indeed. We've provided protection in depth. Notice the clearing behind the fence?'

'You've mined it?' Peter suggested.

'That's only the beginning. Electric mines with doppler radar. The area is covered by concealed machine-gun positions. If the wind is in the right direction, and it usually is — I checked — we're ready to release tear gas.'

'Very nasty mind you have. Don't you know gas is evil?'

'Ya. It keeps them alive. Boiling oil is much better. Besides, it's more traditional.'

Jurgens drove Peter back to the barracks, and Peter grabbed his canvas bag and followed Jurgens into the building.

'Your room,' Jurgens said, stopping before one of the doors. 'Ground floor, eastern exposure, just a short walk from the bath.'

'More than I'd dare hope for,' Peter said, entering the room and tossing his bag on the regulation cot. 'Do I have to sign a lease?'

'No, but we would like the rent in advance. Make yourself at home.'

Peter proceeded to do so.

'What, no pinups?' Jurgens asked as Peter hung his last fatigue uniform in the wall locker and started closing it.

'I carry my adornments on my soul,' Peter said.

The barrack's outer door slammed, and the sound of running feet clattered down the hall. A Bonterre Army private slid to a stop in front of the open door to Peter's room. 'Excuse me, sirs, but I am a runner from the orderly room,' the private panted. 'You are wished at the orderly room. There are guests of importance.'

'Who?' Jurgens asked.

'A Mister Trimam, and, I believe, his daughter.' Message delivered, the private spun around and raced back.

'The ambassador?' asked Peter.

'He's been appointed official civilian liaison with our group,' Jurgens explained as they went down the hall, 'I thought you knew.'

'No. I knew Colonel Lyet had been appointed Army officer in charge, but I didn't know we also rated a civilian.'

'We do, and he's it.'

'Good choice. They're both intelligent men.'

Ambassador Trimam and Marya were waiting on a bench in the orderly room when Peter and Jurgens arrived. The ambassador stood up and shook hands with them. 'It's amazing what you've been able to do in the past three weeks,' he said. 'I was quite impressed with what I saw as we drove in here.'

'Eric will be delighted to give you the guided tour,' said Peter. 'It's good to have you with us. I understand you've been appointed official civilian overseer.'

'Not that exactly,' said Trimam seriously, 'more red tape cutter. My, er, credentials are here.' He pulled a sealed envelope out of his pocket.

Peter took the envelope and looked it over. It was truly sealed, with a wax seal bearing the Royal signet. 'I'm sure you've performed this ceremony in much more imposing surroundings than these,' he said.

'Perhaps, but never in circumstances as important to the welfare of my country.'

'I hope we can live up to our advance billing,' Peter said. 'Come into my office. That is, if I have an office. Have I an office?' he demanded of Jurgens.

'With your name on the door,' Jurgens assured him. 'We couldn't think of a proper title that would be printable, so we settled for your name. Walk this way, please.'

'All hunched over like that? No, thanks, I'll walk properly. But I'll follow you, if you'd care to lead.'

'No, thanks. I'm all booked up for this dance.'

'If you'll excuse my saying so,' Trimam said as they walked down the hall, 'I thought my command of English was quite good, but I seem to be unable to follow your conversation.'

'It's a form of humor, Father,' Marya said. 'A combination of the pun and insult that seems to be peculiarly American.'

'Ah, so,' Trimam said. He looked thoughtful.

'I think we've just been put properly in our place,' Jurgens said. 'Here we are.' He stopped in front of a door with MR. CARTHAGE printed across it in neat, small black letters.

'At least they spelled my name right,' Peter commented, as Jurgens opened the door.

There was an explosion.

Peter felt something slam against his chest, and then he bounced off the opposite wall and hit the floor. A heavy object fell on top of him. It was Jurgens. Marya started to scream.

Peter pulled himself from under Jurgens, and lay still for a second. Except for the chest area, where Jurgens had hit him and he had hit the wall, he felt no pain, but his legs were warm and sticky. His fatigue trousers, he noted in a curiously detached way, were lacerated below the knees, and the warm sticky feeling was blood. He pushed himself up to a sitting position to look at Jurgens.

Jurgens was lying on his back, unconscious but still breathing. The whole front of his uniform was red, and the color deepened as Peter watched. Peter realized that Marya had been screaming when she suddenly stopped. Trimam had clamped his hand over her mouth. She clutched his arm tightly and then, with what seemed a conscious effort of will, shuddered and relaxed.

'Are you all right?' Peter asked.

'Yes,' Trimam said. 'I wasn't touched, and Marya was behind me. How's your friend?' He knelt down beside Jurgens. 'Alive, thank the good Lord.'

'Thank the lack of practice of our friendly bomber. He seems to have planted his bomb too low.'

A crowd of people was gathering in the corridor behind Trimam. 'Will one of you go for a doctor and a stretcher, please?' Peter called.

'Yes, sir,' a sergeant answered. 'The

doctor's on his way now.'

Trimam opened Jurgens' jacket and cut away his undershirt with a penknife. 'Bloody but superficial,' Trimam said, 'at least in the upper part of his body.'

'That's good,' Peter said.

'What about you?' Trimam asked.

'I'm okay, I think. Most of this blood seems to be Eric's.'

A white-garbed figure appeared over Peter's head. 'This must be the place,' he said. 'You must be Colonel Carthage.' He started to examine Jurgens. 'I'm Doctor Petroff. Major Petroff of the Royal Bonterre Army Medical Corps. I hadn't planned to meet you this way.' He put a tourniquet around Jurgens' right leg, and called for the stretcher.

'None the less. Doctor, I'm glad you dropped in,' Peter said as Doctor Petroff turned to him.

'Let's get a look at those legs.' He slit the trousers open, and mopped away some of the blood. 'Minor cuts, you're lucky. We'll bandage you up as good as new.'

'How's Jurgens?'

'He'll be all right. We'll give him some whole blood as a safety measure, I think he'll be up and around in a week or so. Can you stand up?'

'I imagine.' With Doctor Petroff's assistance, Peter climbed to his feet.

'Fine. Come over to the dispensary and I'll finish cleaning you up.' Petroff turned to Trimam and his daughter. 'Are you two all right?'

'Yes,' Trimam said, 'no damage.'

Marya nodded.

'I guess that none of that blood's yours, then.'

Trimam looked down. His pants were splattered with blood. 'Not mine,' he assured the doctor.

Leaving Ambassador Trimam and Marya in the hands off Tony Ryan, who had just walked into the building, Peter went to the dispensary to get bandaged up, and then to his room to clean up and change clothes. He returned to the headquarters building about forty minutes later.

All the damage to the hall had been cleared away by this time, but the floor was stained, the door to his office was missing and the interior of the room was a hopeless mess.

'It was such a nice door,' he complained to Ryan in the latter's office, 'with my name on it and everything.'

'We'll see that you get a new one,' Ryan assured him.

'That'd be good of you. Whatever happened to that envelope?' he asked Trimam.

'It ended up on the floor, and I retrieved it. It's a bit smudged.' He handed the envelope over.

'It is a bit smudged,' Peter agreed, examining the blood-and-dirt-smeared envelope. 'I hope we don't make a general practice of this.' He ripped the envelope open and glanced at the document inside. 'Is there any formal way I'm supposed to accept your credentials?' he asked Trimam. 'I'm rather new at this.'

'You could make a speech,' Trimam told him, 'but on the whole . . . '

'I quite agree,' Tony Ryan said. 'Let's not have him make a speech . . . Incidentally, old man, did it occur to you that someone's trying to kill you?'

'Something like that had crossed my mind,' Peter agreed. 'I wonder who has my welfare so much at heart?'

Ambassador Trimam exchanged glances with Marya, who shrugged her exquisite shoulders.

'Here,' Tomy said, 'I have something for you to look at.'

'What's this?' Peter took the manila folder, which had 'Operational Top Secret' stamped in red across the front, holding it gingerly as though it might contain another bomb.

'The week's report to Steadman. Approve it, so we can send it out.'

'Ah!' Peter opened the folder and settled down to read the three typewritten pages. 'Very good,' he said a minute later.

'You finished it already?'

'I'm a fast reader. Have this coded and sent out.'

'Just initial the first page for me, there's a good boy.'

Peter added his initials to those of the other section heads, and turned to Ambassador Trimam. 'If we're supposed to be working together, there's no reason for you not to read this, if you're interested.'

'Yes,' Trimam assented, 'I'd be very interested.' He took the document from Peter's hand and started to read.

'The coded copy's right here,' Tony said, fishing another paper out of his desk. 'We're nothing if not efficient. Bob Alvin has his computer set up to do the coding and decoding at the push of a button. We'll get it to the telegraph office in Bonterre this afternoon.'

'I'll take it in,' Peter offered. 'I've got to go into the city this afternoon anyway.'

'You'd almost think,' Ambassador Trimam commented, looking up from the paper, 'that this is already in code. It's full of abbreviations that have no meaning to me, and words that seem to be used in new meanings.'

'We've got our own jargon,' Peter said. 'I can see where it might puzzle anyone new to it. What don't you understand?' Peter spent the next ten minutes explaining the various shorthand terms and acronyms used in the report.

'Aha!' Professor Perlemutter stalked into the room. 'Ambassador Trimam, I'm glad you're here. I'm doing a study of various habits and customs of the people of your charming country, and I could use your assistance in evaluating some of my information. It's much easier to find out the customs than to make any sort of judgment as to their relative importance.'

'What sort of thing do you mean?' Trimam asked.

'Well, take for example superstition. Astrology seems to be firmly entrenched among the natives, but of what importance is it to them — how seriously do they take it?'

'Very seriously, I'm afraid,' Trimam said. 'Some of our most enlightened and highly placed officials wouldn't take any action without first making sure that the moment is astrologically auspicious.'

'Interesting,' Perlemutter said, rubbing his hands together, 'fascinating. Could I take you away for about an hour and pick your mind of such details? Have you an hour to spare?'

'Gladly,' Trimam said, laughing. 'You'll probably teach me more about our customs than I know myself.'

'I have to go back,' said Marya. 'His

Majesty said he'd need me this after-noon.'

'I'm leaving in a few minutes. It'd be a pleasure to drive you back to the place,' Peter offered.

'Thank you, Mister Carthage.' Marya smiled and the room became brighter.

'Then it's settled,' her father said. 'I'll see you at home this evening.'

Peter drove the staff car toward Bonterre with half his attention on driv-ing, and half on the beautiful girl sitting beside him. Marya of the exquisitely deli-cate looks was also proving to have a high degree of intelligence and inquisitiveness.

The questions she asked showed that she had kept herself informed of the politi-cal and military situation in Bonterre, and understood what she read. Peter only half noticed when the conversation switched to details of his personal life.

'How long were you in the American Army, Mister Carthage?' Marya asked.

'If you keep calling me 'Mister Carthage,' and I keep replying with 'Miss Trimam,' we're going to sound like characters out of a Victorian novel. My

137

first name is Peter, and I'd like to hear how it sounds when you say it.'

'Peter.' Marya made music out of the name. 'Very good. You may call me Marya.' A complex tone poem.

Peter laughed. 'Marya,' he said. 'I won't try to imitate what it sounds like when you say it, but it's a beautiful name.'

'Peter and Marya. How long were you in the American Army, Peter?'

'I went in during the Korean War, got a battlefield commission, and transferred to the intelligence branch after the war. Somehow, I stayed in.'

'Did you go to college?'

'After the war. I'd had two years before, and I managed to persuade the Army to send me back.'

'And then?'

'And then I became one of the small cogs in the Army machine. There I was, immured, thinking life had nothing better to offer, until two years ago when I joined War, Incorporated.'

'It's better than the Army?'

Peter smiled. 'Life has nothing better to offer,' he said.

'You compress the story of your life so,' Marya told him seriously. 'All the details which have formed the pattern that gives meaning to your life have been left out. What you mention are the directions your life has taken, but you've omitted the signposts that caused you to choose these directions.'

Peter considered that for a minute, while negotiating the car between two heavily laden carts whose drivers had stopped to yell at each other. 'That's interesting,' he said. 'You're right, but I never thought of it before. I imagine most people never analyze the reason they do anything. Important turnings in a person's life can usually be stated without being questioned. 'I joined the Army.' 'I became a lawyer.' 'I got married.' Maybe the reasons are too involved with emotion to discuss. Or, perhaps, they're just too trite.'

'Are you married?' Marya asked.

'I was,' Peter said. He waited for the question, but Marya asked it only with a continued silence. 'It was in my last year of school,' he continued finally. 'She was in my class, but about four years younger than me. Joan. A pretty, vivacious, intelligent girl. It lasted a little over a year. We were incompatible.'

'That's one of those words,' Marya said softly.

'Yes,' Peter agreed. 'One of those beautiful, imprecise words that can mean whatever you want it to. What it meant in our case . . .

'After graduation the Army sent me to an intelligence school outside of Washington for six months. We had a nice little apartment in West Virginia, and Joan was becoming a nice little Army wife. She joined the clubs the other little Army wives belonged to; we threw the obligatory parties for the other officers and their wives. She was a perfect First. Lieutenant's Wife, looking forward to becoming a perfect Captain's Wife, and someday, perhaps, a perfect General's Wife. She had found her niche.'

'And one day you found out she wasn't perfect?' Marya suggested. 'Another man?'

'Joan?' Peter said savagely. 'Don't be silly. That would have meant drama, excitement, disorder. No, it wasn't anything as positive as that. It was much simpler. When the course was over I got my orders. I was being sent to Ethiopia, and not even to the embassy, but to a little place in the hills. Part of a team of some three officers and twenty enlisted men on a special assignment that would take about a year. Oh, it was quite safe, and all that. A lot of the men brought their wives. Do you see?'

'No,' Marya answered, sounding puzzled. 'I see nothing.'

'That's what Joan saw,' Peter said, 'nothing. No officers' wives to play bridge with, no club, not even a PX. She refused to go. We had quite a scene, the only fight I remember us having. I couldn't get my orders changed, and wouldn't have if I could. So I went, and she stayed. Three months later I got my first letter from her. In it were the papers she wanted me to sign for the divorce.'

Marya touched his arm. 'I'm sorry,' she said. 'You still — feel for her?'

'Nonsense,' Peter barked. 'That was years ago.'

'Yes? Of course . . . You're going a bit fast for this road.'

'What?' Peter took his foot off the accelerator, and slowed the car from seventy to forty. 'Sorry. Maybe I do get a bit emotional when I talk about her.'

'The lives of the men working under you must have been hell for a few months.' Marya smiled.

'They were a very independent group,' Peter remembered, 'I never could have gotten away with anything like that.'

The car was now entering the outskirts of Bonterre, and traffic was starting to pick up. Bonterre drivers had a strong tendency to be erratic, having no apparent regard for the concept of right of way, or even the correct side of the road. Peter had to devote more of his attention to driving, and the conversation died off.

'Would you mind if I stop at the telegraph office before I drop you?' Peter asked.

'That's fine with me,' Marya said. 'I'm still early.' Peter parked the car in front of the telegraph office. 'I'll be a few minutes,' he told Marya. 'Do you want to wait in the car?'

'I'll come with you,' Marya said, 'if you don't mind.'

'Of course not,' Peter assured her. He helped her out of the car, and she linked arms with him and started toward the telegraph office.

As they entered the office, they were almost knocked down by Richard Logan, who seemed in a hurry to leave. 'Mister Logan,' Peter said politely.

'Yes. Fancy meeting you here. Sorry I bumped into you.'

'Of course,' Peter agreed.

'We'll have to have another long talk sometime,' Logan said. 'Goodbye, Miss Trimam.' He tipped an imaginary hat to Marya, and slammed through tlie door.

'He seems to be in an awful hurry,' Marya said.

'He seems to be angry,' Peter commented. 'I wonder if he always seems to be angry.'

Peter walked over to the counter and stared at the clerk, who studiously ignored him for two minutes. In Bonterre it's considered bad form to wait on anyone when he first comes in. It would be a sign of low status to be so innocent of things to do that you're immediately available.

After the requisite two-minute waiting period, the clerk recognized Peter's existence and came over to the counter. 'May I assist you?' he asked.

'I'd like to have this telegram sent out today, if that's possible.' Peter spread the pages of five-letter code groups on the counter.

'Of course,' the clerk agreed. 'Would you please insert the message onto the correct form, of which you will find a pad on the table behind you?'

'We've been sending telegrams on this form for the past three weeks,' Peter pointed out.

'Of course,' the clerk said. 'Correct form has just been put in stock. Your message is on old form, which is obsolete, and may no longer be used.'

'Well,' Peter said, realizing the uselessness of arguing with the bureaucratic mind, 'it's an honest mistake. I'll copy my message onto the correct form for you right now, so I can still get it out tonight.'

'Of course,' the clerk said. 'Is necessary. Other American gentleman argue for half an hour before he believe there is nothing I can do about new regulation concerning correct form.'

'I noticed that he seemed angry as he left,' Peter said.

'Very stubborn gentleman,' the clerk told Peter.

Peter went over to the table and pulled the pad of 'correct forms' over to him. The top page was deeply indented where someone had pressed heavily on the sheet over it with a bail-point pen, and the marks had come through. 'Aha!' Peter said, his Sherlock Holmes instinct roused. He held the paper up at an angle, and peered across it. 'That's funny.'

'What's so amusing?' Marya asked.

'Our Mister Logan seems to be sending coded messages too.' He showed Marya how to hold the paper so as to make out the writing.

'What does that mean?' Marya asked.

'I refuse to make deductions from

insufficient evidence,' Peter said. 'It's too easy to be proven wrong. I do think, however, that it's safe to say that this bears further looking into.' He ripped the page off the pad and carefully put it into an inside pocket.

'Mister Logan's a spy!'

'Mister Logan is probably no more than a prudent businessman,' Peter told Marya. 'Don't let your sense of the dramatic run away with itself.' He addressed himself to the task of copying his coded text onto the new forms.

'I think he's a spy,' Marya insisted.

10

The coffee in the paper cup tasted, as usual, like hot, sweet mud. It came from an automatic dispenser that had been set up in the orderly room.

Peter put the cup down and pushed it away from him across the desk. 'This stuff's unconstitutional,' he said. 'Something about cruel and unusual punishments.'

'I don't know about cruel,' Tony said from the other side of the desk, 'but I'll go along with the unusual.'

'Well, it's a present from the Old Man, so I guess we'll just have to learn to live with it. He'd probably take it as a personal insult if we junked that machine and got an old-fashioned coffee urn.'

The door to the office opened and closed. 'John Wander,' Tony said without turning to look.

Wander, who had just come through the door, focused on Ryan through his black-framed glasses. 'Very good,' he said.

'Now I'm supposed to ask you how you knew without looking, and you'll make some clever remark about how my pipe tobacco stinks.'

'It, er, does have a certain distinct aroma about it,' Tony admitted.

'What do you need, John?' Peter asked before the conversation could continue any further in the direction it seemed to be heading.

'Need?' Wander took the pipe out of his mouth. 'Oh, yes. No needs, I've got some news for you. That telegraph form you gave me last week, I set up an iodine vapor gadget, used bottled iodine from the dispensary. It works very well.'

'Yes, and . . . ?'

'And we got all the writing off it. Five-letter code groups. Gave a copy to the computer boys to play with, see if they can come up with anything. Interesting thing, though, the cover address is in our file. The,' he consulted a piece of paper, 'Pacific Area Trade Council, San Francisco. It's listed as a known CIA drop.'

'The Agency,' Peter mused. 'So he's

one of their boys. It figures.'

'Professor Perlemutter had a talk with one of the telegraph clerks, and we now have a complete back file of everything Logan sent since he got here. Computer section says they have at least an even chance of breaking the crypt.'

'How'd Perlemutter manage that?' Peter asked. 'From what I saw of the clerks they seemed comparatively graft-free and excessively regulation-conscious.'

'The professor has his methods, but they must remain forever as mysteries to us mere mortal men. Well, I hope that's of some use. I've got to get back to work.' Nodding to Peter and Tony, John Wander left the office.

'Marya was right,' Peter commented.

'What's that?' Ryan asked.

'She said Logan was a spy, and a spy he is.'

'What do you suggest we do about it?'

'Do? Nothing. It's a piece of information that'll come in handy, but I can't think of any particular course of action to take on it.'

'Okay,' Tony said. 'We'll just take it

under advisement, as they say.'

The telephone on Peter's desk rang, and he grabbed for it. 'Yes?' After a second he said, 'It's Jurgens' to Tony, and then went back to the conversation.

When he had hung up Tony glared at him and said, 'Well?'

'He's getting out of the hospital later today.'

'That's great news. When can he get back to work?'

'I guess, tomorrow.'

'Great. Then I can give up teaching the tactics course.'

'I didn't realize you'd taken it over.'

'Yup. And I've been teaching it Jurgens' style, so he shouldn't have any trouble taking it back.'

'Jurgens' style? I know better, but I'll ask anyway. What do you call Jurgens' style?'

'Sort of on a primitive level. Like the advice a football coach gives his team before the game. You know, 'Hit 'em hard, hit 'em low, hit 'em fast, and if they get up, hit 'em again.''

'I think you underrate Jurgens a little.'

'I admit to a slight exaggeration. Where's Colonel Lyet? I thought he was supposed to meet us here.'

'He's not late yet,' Peter said, glancing at his watch. 'He has another two minutes.'

Precisely two minutes later, Colonel Lyet was ushered into the office by a lieutenant on duty in the orderly room. 'Good morning, gentlemen. Mister Carthage, I understand you're an expert diver, is that right?'

'I've used scuba equipment in my life,' Peter admitted cautiously. 'What do you have in mind?'

'The Bonterre Air Force sank something off the coast last night, a small boat of some kind, and I think it might be of some use to take a look at it.'

'The whole Air Force?' Ryan asked.

'All three planes of it,' Colonel Lyet agreed.

'What makes you think that whatever they sank is worth going out to take a look at?' Peter asked.

'There are several factors,' Lyet told them. He counted off the factors on his fingers.

'First, it's the first we've known of guerrillas operating by boat. Second, they're in an unusual location. Third, it was sunk close enough offshore so that it's easily reachable by diving. Fourth, it's the first thing the Air Force has ever sunk, so they'd like to know more about it.'

'How'd the Air Force know it was a guerrilla boat?' Ryan asked.

'At first they didn't. They were on a routine patrol and one of the pilots went down for a closer look at the boat. At least, that's the way he wrote it in his report. Personally, I think he just buzzed the craft out of boredom. Anyway, they opened up on him with twin twenty-millimeter machine guns, so he decided they were hostile.'

'They must have thought he was on to them,' Peter said.

'So. Between the three planes they managed to sink the boat. It must have been quite a shock to them, somebody firing back. From the way they've been carrying on, you'd think they'd sunk the whole Seventh Fleet.'

'It might be worth taking a look at,'

Peter decided. 'Where's this thing sunk?'

'Some miles north of Tabala. Right off the main section of the DuMarte plantation.'

'Have you got any scuba gear?'

'I was hoping you people would have brought some with you. I thought you were planning to give a course in diving.'

'That's right, but I don't know if the equipment's here yet.'

'I think it is,' Tony Ryan offered, 'I'll check.' He made a phone call. 'It's in supply now. Or, at any rate one set of gear is. We're supposed to get twelve, but only one's come in so far.'

'One will do,' Peter said. 'I rarely wear more than one at a time.'

'Gosh,' Tony said. 'I had hopes of going down with you and fighting off the minions of the enemy while you rescued either the H-bomb or the beautiful heroine, depending on what chapter this is.'

'Sorry about that,' Peter said.

The DuMarte plantation main house, which except for the surrounding rubber trees could have come straight out of

Gone With the Wind, presented the Ionic columns of its front entrance at the end of a long, wide driveway. By the time the jeep had reached the house, Mme. DuMarte was waiting on the porch steps, the picture of the perfect hostess in a light, cotton print dress. 'Good afternoon, gentlemen,' she greeted them as they got out of the jeep, 'what can I do for you?'

Before she would allow them to answer the question, she brought them into the house and had drinks served. 'In a gentler age,' she told them, 'I would be serving tea. But I'm not at all sure that I would have enjoyed living in a gentler age.'

Peter sat in an armchair, while Colonel Lyet and Tony Ryan occupied opposite ends of an ornate couch. Mme. DuMarte faced Peter in a high-backed armchair. The grouping of couch and armchairs was in a semicircle around a large fireplace. The style of the room was, fittingly enough, French Provincial, and expensive. The rack of rifles above the fireplace struck the only jarring note.

'This room would have been quite in place in that gentler age, Madame

DuMarte,' Peter said. 'It's very impressive.'

'Do call me Annette, all of you. Please. Yes, this room is for show. My husband was quite proud of it. And now, gentlemen, how may I help you?'

'Madame DuMarte,' Colonel Lyet leaned forward, 'have you been bothered by the guerrillas?'

Annette DuMarte laced her fingers together, with her elbows resting on the arms of the chair, and rested her chin on the arch thus formed. Her blonde hair casually framed her face. Her full breasts were separately outlined in the confines of the light cotton dress. Peter was suddenly very aware of her as a woman, and he had the feeling that she knew, and approved.

'No, I haven't been seriously bothered by the guerrilla forces. A few minor harassments, but that's all. It puzzles me. As one of the principal landowners m Bonterre, I would expect to have been more favored with their attentions.'

'It's not really so strange,' Peter said, leaning back in his chair and enjoying his view of Annette DuMarte as he spoke.

155

'The guerrillas usually try to consolidate their position with the peasants in an area before starting raids on the landowners.'

'That won't be easy around here,' Annette said. 'My husband was a very generous and liberal man. The natives employed by the plantation and in the surrounding towns are very loyal to the DuMarte interests.'

'The guerrillas have ways to break down loyalty,' Colonel Lyet said. 'They replace it with fear. A few well-timed murders can do a lot in that direction.'

'If any such program has been started in the area, I am as yet unaware of it,' Annette told the colonel.

'Let's hope you continue to stay lucky,' Tony said, sipping his drink.

'We came to see you,' Colonel Lyet said, 'Concerning the sinking of a small boat offshore last night.'

'You mean the cabin cruiser your planes sank with their machine guns? Yes. I saw it from my boat dock.'

'It was a cabin cruiser, you say?' the colonel asked. 'It was too dark for the pilots to identify for sure.'

'Ah, then it was an accident — a chance happening — I thought so. Yes. One of the planes swooped down very low over the boat, and the people in the boat started firing at it. I thought at the time that if it was a rebel — guerrilla — boat, it was a silly thing to do, as the planes would have no way of telling. Then the planes started strafing the boat until they had sunk it. It took them six passes.'

'Ah, so. That wasn't in their report, I thank you. What we desire from you is permission to examine the sunken boat.'

'How can I refuse?' Annette asked. 'However, although the water is shallow offshore, it's hardly that shallow. The boat must be about ten meters down.'

'I've brought some diving equipment,' Peter told her, 'and I'd like to go down for a close look.'

'We're very curious about what the guerrillas were carrying in the boat,' Tony added.

'Very good,' Annette said. 'I'll come with you. We'll go down to the boat house and take out the cruiser. I think I can point out just about where the boat went down.'

'We'd appreciate that,' Peter said. 'One of the pilots marked the approximate location on a chart for us, but you could probably give us a better fix than that if you were watching.'

'I was indeed,' Annette said. 'The last time I saw anything like that was during World War Two, and I was quite young at the time.'

'It must have been quite a show,' Tony said.

'I suppose it was, if you like that sort of thing. The idea of one group of men killing another, for whatever reason, has never appealed to me.' Annette spoke softly, but with conviction. 'Now, if you gentlemen will wait a moment while I change, we'll go down to the water.' She got up from her chair and left the room with the self-assured grace of a queen.

'An admirable woman,' Colonel Lyet said, as the door closed behind her.

'She's all of that,' Peter agreed.

When Annette came back into the room she had a beach robe draped around her shoulders. Under the open robe her well-tanned body, concealed only by the briefest of bathing suits, glistened slightly as she walked. There was a sensuousness about her, a very female awareness of her body and its effect on men. Peter noted her flat stomach and her well-muscled thighs, and wondered what she'd be like in bed. Annette DuMarte was a woman — and, Peter thought, she enjoyed being a woman.

'Shall we go?' Annette asked.

The group got into the jeep, with Tony driving and Colonel Lyet sitting beside him. Peter and Annette shared the back with the scuba equipment. When the jeep went around a turn, Annette grabbed Peter's arm to steady herself. She made no attempt to remove her hand after that, but softly caressed Peter's arm in an absent-minded way that fooled neither of them.

The jeep pulled up in front of the boat house, a large, unpainted wooden structure half in the water, with a short pier jutting out from one side. Annette jumped out of the jeep and, pulling a large key from her robe, attacked the padlock on the door. Peter and Tony unloaded the scuba gear from the jeep.

Annette swung the wide boat house doors open, revealing a large, white cabin cruiser riding gently at the dock. The name, *Le Noceur*, was painted in black script on the prow.

'The Roisterer,' Tony translated, 'happy name for a boat.'

'It was my husband's favorite toy,' Annette said. She went to the back of the boat house and, after opening another padlock, pulled in the chain that kept the boat penned from the sea.

Peter and Tony put the scuba gear down on the polished mahogany deck, and Annette started the powerful diesel engine. Backing the craft carefully out of the shed, she turned it around and reversed the engine. *Le Noceur* shot forward. The sea was a calm, transparent blue which, with the deep blue of the sky, neatly framed the green jungle that crept out to the water's edge.

Colonel Lyet took a map out of his briefcase and, sitting on deck in a wooden folding chair, spread it open across his knees.

'Don't worry about that, Colonel,'

Annette called from the wheel, 'I'll take you right to the place.'

The boat moved smoothly across the water while Peter stripped down to the bathing suit he was wearing under his uniform. Tony helped him adjust the scuba tanks on his back.

Annette cut the boat's engine to an idle, allowing *Le Noceur* to gently bob up and down in the bay. 'It should be about here,' she said.

Colonel Lyet checked several landmarks on shore through a small sighting compass, carefully triangulated his findings on the map, and nodded in agreement. 'This is just about where the pilot puts it.'

'Could you please take over the wheel, Mister Ryan?' Annette asked. 'I have a scuba outfit in the cabin, and I think I'd like to go down with Mister Carthage.'

'Of course,' Tony said.

'I don't know . . . ' Peter started.

'I'm an expert diver,' Annette told him. 'Be back in a moment.' She disappeared into the cabin. In a minute she returned with a scuba tank on her well-tanned back. Pausing for a moment to adjust the rubberized canvas straps which criss-crossed bare skin and bright-red bikini, she joined Peter by the rail. 'Off to find sunken treasure,' she said.

'Recently sunken treasure,' Peter agreed.

Together they climbed over the railing and down the side of the boat, gradually lowering themselves into the bay. The water was cold at first, but in a few seconds they were used to it. 'You'd better have some towels ready for us,' Peter called to Tony, 'we'll be freezing when we come out.'

'Will do,' Tony answered. 'Have fun.'

Peter adjusted the face mask and breathing tube, hung his speargun across his chest, and nodded at Annette. She nodded back, and gave the thumbs up sign.

They sank beneath the surface of the bay. Peter took the lead, his muscular legs working in a scissor motion, the webbed flippers pushing him steadily forward and down toward the coral ledge that formed the bottom. Annette stayed close behind him and to the right, in approved spearfishing style, her speargun held ready in her right hand.

They were almost to the bottom before the sunlight began to desert them. The water took on a gloomy quality, the meager light seeming to come from all directions and lighting everything equally. There were no shadows on the bottom, which seemed brightly lit directly below but receded into vagueness at a distance of a few feet. The coral formations, which seemed a uniform light gray from a distance, took on color from a foot away. Delicate pinks, pastel shades of blue and green and occasional vivid splashes of red came into view as they swam slowly along the bottom, then receded into gray again a few feet behind them.

As always when diving, Peter had the feeling of having entered a different world, as alien from the earth above him as Mars or Venus, and for a large part as little understood or explored.

Annette swam up to him in the silence and reached out for his hand. They swam together this way for some time, a line of bubbles to the surface marking their progress in the search for the sunken cabin cruiser. The larger fish carefully avoided them. A few of the smaller fish swam along with them for a while and then, their curiosity satisfied, wandered off again. Once a twelve-foot shark lazily paralleled their course some distance above them, and all other fish disappeared, but the shark too went on its way without bothering the intruders. A school of several thousand fish, each about two inches long and colored like a Japanese print, swam up to them, parted, and swam around them without bothering to notice their existence. We've just been passed by a university, Peter thought, and then felt annoyed because he couldn't tell Annette.

When they swam over a coral hill, they suddenly came upon the cabin cruiser resting on the other side. It was right side up, leaning to port, and the damage inflicted by the fifty-caliber guns of Bonterre's Air Force was very evident on the hull. Whole planks were stove in, and it was riddled with holes ranging from one to three inches in diameter. The weight of the lead it picked up alone would be enough to sink it, Peter thought as they swam over to the wreck.

Annette went around to the front of the boat, while Peter examined the deck and then made his way into the closed cabin. The deck and cabin were bare, except for the fittings that came with the boat. There wasn't even a bed in the cabin. There were no bodies in the ship. They must have all been on deck, Peter thought, and they either got killed and floated off, or swam to shore. On the floor of the cabin were four large crates. One of them was split open. Peter took the flashlight off his belt and directed its beam into the crate. It was packed with rifles. He took one out of the crate and examined it. It was identical to the one that had been fired at him from the top of the building.

Two of the other crates were similar to the broken one, the fourth was different. Peter worked it free, and managed to pry off one of the boards. It was full of what appeared to be precision hand tools. He examined two of the tools before their use became evident to him. It was reloading equipment for rifle bullets. Enough to equip a small hand-operated ammunition factory.

Peter was still staring at the tool collection when Annette came swimming through the cabin door. She regarded his discoveries with a critical eye for a moment, and then started exploring the rest of the cabin. A minute later she poked at him and gestured upward. He floated to the top of the cabin with her, wondering what she had found, and then his head came out of the wafer. There was an air pocket about a foot and a half deep at the top of the cabin. Peter cautiously took the breathing tube out of his mouth and tested the air in the submerged pocket. Aside from a strong salt smell, the air was good. Peter took off his mask.

Annette took off her own mask and sniffed the air. 'It was good of the boat to leave some air for us when it sank,' she said.

'Very considerate,' Peter agreed, his words echoing hollowly in the confined space.

Annette licked her lips. 'It seems to me that some use should be made of this unexpected good fortune,' she said, putting her arms around Peter's neck.

'What do you have in mind?' Peter asked.

She kissed him. When they paused for breath, she asked, 'Have you ever made love underwater?'

'No,' Peter said, pulling her close and resuming the interrupted kiss.

'Good,' she said, kissing his right eye. 'Neither have I,' she continued, nibbling at his ear. 'I like novelty.' She placed her lips again on his, and pulled their bodies together in a satisfying and imaginative manner.

At length they were spent, and they rested together six fathoms below the surface of the water. 'Peter!' Annette said, testing the sound of his name while kissing his shoulders and neck.

'I think the air's getting bad,' Peter said pragmatically.

Annette laughed, and the sound echoed in their small chamber. She reached for the two scraps of red fabric, transformed them again into a bathing suit, and began adjusting her scuba equipment. 'I suppose we'd better return to the real world upstairs.'

Peter put on his bathing suit, and strapped the scuba tank over it. 'They're probably starting to worry about us.' He picked up one of the rifles from the case, kissed Annette, and put on his mask.

The trip to the surface was uneventful, and they emerged from the water about two hundred yards from the boat. By the time they swam over, Tony and Colonel Lyet were at the rail waiting.

'You had us worried,' Tony said. 'By our figuring your air supply should have run out about fifteen minutes ago.'

'We found an air pocket in the ship,' Peter said. He tossed the rifle on deck. 'Here, a sample of the cargo.' He helped Annette up, and then clambered over the rail himself.

'What happened to your back?' Tony asked.

'Coral,' Peter explained.

'I think I'll go down to the cabin to dry off,' Annette said.

Laughing at something that neither Tony nor the colonel could figure out, Peter dried himself with a giant towel while the boat roared back to shore.

11

The hut stood in the middle of a rain forest, with no clearing around it to mark its presence and no path to lead the curious to its door. It was built low to the ground, and overhanging trees effectively shielded it from the prying eyes of low-flying observation planes. Using infrared film, a trained analyst might find it as a slight blob of heat in the otherwise ever-cold forest. If he was lucky enough to take the picture on the one or two days a month that the hut was occupied, he might get a clear enough reading from the concentration of human body heat to interpret it accurately. But it was highly unlikely.

On this day the hut was occupied. Four people stood in its gloomy interior. Behind a tall screen in one corner stood X, a person whose identity was unknown even to the others in the room. In front of the screen, unconsciously huddled together as primitive man might when facing the unknown, were three representatives of the Bonterre People's Volunteer Rebel Army: Comrade General Lin Tsui, military commander of the guerrilla force, Comrade Commissar Bun Kee Tappa of the political arm, and Colonel Tchin Op, liaison officer to General Tsui.

In a thin, high, childlike voice, which effectively concealed age and sex, X greeted the guerrilla leaders in flawless French: 'You have come.'

'So,' General Tsui spoke. 'It is good that you called this meeting. We have something to discuss with you.'

'Speak.'

General Tsui glared at the screen. 'We had bargained for a shipment of guns at the usual terms. For an exorbitant extra amount we were to also receive the tools necessary to reload rifle ammunition.'

'Are you here,' X interrupted, 'to bicker about the price?'

'Not that. We agreed to your suggestion as to how the delivery was to be made. Our ship met your agent on the coast and he guided it to the pickup point. Immediately after the pickup was made, the ship was attacked by government aircraft. It was only by the greatest good fortune that our men were able to escape and come back with the story of what happened.'

'Bah,' the figure behind the screen snorted, 'your men are fools!'

'Perhaps, but we are not such fools as to be blind to betrayal! How did the planes know to attack that boat?'

'What makes you think the planes did know?'

'A question cannot be answered by a question,' Commissar Tappa said softly. 'And what is self-evident cannot be talked away. The planes attacked a boat. They attacked the right boat. Therefore, and with the greatest reluctance, we are forced to conclude that they had prior knowledge of which boat to attack.'

'A question cannot answer a question,' X replied in the voice of a child, 'but it might cause you to think — a welcome novelty — and thus discover the information you seek in the knowledge you already have. Are you suggesting that I betrayed you?'

171

'No,' General Tsui answered, 'but only because it would be against your own self-interest, not because of any feeling of loyalty you have for the cause.'

'Don't be more infantile than you can help,' came the somehow-dangerous sounding voice. 'I claim no more liking for your dictatorship of a 'People's Democracy' than for the kakistocracy of a republican government now in power. That isn't, and never has been, the point. I, and the group I represent, support you because you can help us in what we're doing. That is so now, and has not changed.'

'A traitor in your organization?' Commissar Tappa suggested.

'Not so.'

'You have never told us why you support us,' General Tsui said, 'but we have our own ideas; and those ideas make it clear that it is not just for what we supply you with, and one day you will find it no longer in your interest to aid us. But we would not like to believe that day is yet come.'

'I will tell you what happened with the boat,' the figure behind the screen said, 'and if you question your men carefully, you will be able to get them to admit that it is so.

'One of the aircraft flew down low over the water to take a close look at the boat. The pilot had no idea that it was crewed by members of the People's Volunteer Rebel Army — or, in this case, perhaps Navy? — when he flew over. One of your men panicked and started to fire at the plane with the machine guns that were so unwisely hidden on the deck. After that rash act it would have been difficult to keep the pilots from guessing that the boat below them was not something other than it looked.'

Commissar Tappa turned to the general, 'Could this be so?'

'I will look into it,' the general said.

'You will find that it is as I have stated,' X snapped. 'Are there any further complaints before we get down to business?'

'No,' General Tsui said. 'The 'business,' I suppose, consists of your informing us that we have to pay for the shipment despite the fact that we did not receive it.'

'It was in the hands of your men before it was so foolishly delivered to the bottom of the ocean. But I will not quibble. I am prepared to replace the weapons you lost, this time without increasing your expense. I am even ready to break one of my own rules and deliver the weapons to you here. I cannot, now, replace the reloading equipment, but I will see that it is in the next shipment, for the same fee. That is my offer.'

'Then we only have to pay twice for the tools, a most generous offer.'

'Yes, since your stupidity lost the first shipment. We think it is most generous indeed. If such a thing happens again, rest assured that you will pay in full for the replacement of the shipment.'

'I will check your information,' the general said, 'and if it is as you say, it will not happen again.'

'You have brought the agreed payment?'

Colonel Op looked at the general, who nodded. The colonel went to the door of the hut and gestured. Four men appeared carrying a large chest. They brought it inside and set it in the center of the room.

A heavy smell filled the air. General Tsui snapped the two hasps with the sound of double gunshots and swung the massive lid opened. The chest was filled with a reddish-brown substance with the consistency of tar. The heavy, bitter smell cloyed the nostrils of those in the room until they could almost taste it.

'Opium,' Commissar Tappa said. 'Two hundred pounds of raw opium. A good price for four times the number of guns you deliver.'

'If you can do better,' X said, 'I shan't hold you back. Sell it elsewhere.'

'We do,' Commissar Tappa said, 'you know that. Most of the drug used in Bonterre is supplied by us. Much as we dislike the trade, we do what we must. What we wonder is where you use this.'

'But Commissar,' the high voice answered, 'I thought you had guessed. We don't sell in Bonterre, and we don't deal in opium.'

'So?'

'Heroin is so much more transportable, and there's such a demand for it in Europe and America.'

'So you have your own factory?'

'Yes. We convert your bulky, sticky mass of opium into neat little packets of white powder. So much more esthetic.'

'And even more habit-forming,' the general said.

'A pity,' X agreed. At an unseen signal four natives entered through a back door. They put the chest on their shoulders and departed as they had come. 'I am leaving now,' X stated. 'You will be notified of our next meeting the usual way. The guns are behind this screen.'

There was a slight rustling noise, and then the guerrillas were alone in the room.

* * *

'I'm glad you decided to come with me,' Marya told Peter as the jeep bounced over the dirt road. 'I've had no one to practice on.'

'Practice?' Peter asked, knowing it was a mistake.

'My driving. I've just learned, you know.'

'No, I didn't.' Peter winced as Marya

went gaily over a large rut. 'Although, I suppose I should have guessed.'

'Oh? What does that mean?'

'Your general air of — enthusiasm — should have told me that you haven't been driving long enough for it to get to be a habit.'

'I see,' Marya said, furiously concentrating on the road. She kept her petite figure hunched forward in the seat, and peered determinedly over the wheel.

After watching for a while, Peter decided that she did better when she concentrated less. 'Exactly what is this event we're tearing at breakneck speed to get to?' he asked.

'The fair? It's traditional. Nobody knows exactly how many years Badabba has held a fair every spring,' Marya told him.

Peter spent the next minute sorting the sentence out. 'It's called the King's fair,' Marya continued, 'because the King opens it with a speech every year. It's part of the tradition.'

'What do they sell at the fair?'

'Oh, you know — cows, pigs, things

like that. And, of course, the King's sandals.'

'The King's sandals?'

'Yes. Oh, not a pair he's worn. He donates a pair of sandals to the fair to be auctioned off for charity. It's . . . '

' . . . Traditional, I know.'

'That's right.' Marya frowned. 'You shouldn't make fun of tradition.'

'I wasn't,' Peter assured her.

'For instance, that uniform you're wearing looks the way it does only through tradition,' Marya said positively.

'No more so than your dress,' Peter commented, looking appreciatively at the thin cotton print that did such nice things for the slender body it covered.

'There aren't millions of people wearing dresses identical to mine,' Marya stated, pursuing her thought.

'There aren't nearly that many women with good enough figures.'

'That's not what I meant,' Marya said, flushing. She silently guided the jeep over the ruts for a minute, and then rallied to the attack. 'Your uniform,' she persisted. 'It's the same as the Bonterre Army and the American Army, but War, Inc.'s a private company. Why's that, if not tradition?'

'Surplus,' Peter told her.

'What do you mean?'

'Army surplus. This is the United States Army tropical worsted uniform, a version of the khaki. The Army has millions of them made up to prepare for wars we don't fight, and then sells them as surplus. After a while we fight the war anyway, and the Army has to have more millions of uniforms made up.'

'Why does War, Inc., use the uniform?' Marya asked.

'Since it buys them surplus, it gets them cheap. Actually, we all buy our own. The patches and brass are supplied by the company.'

'Brass?'

Peter indicated the two emblems on the lapels of his jacket, three letters done in silver: WAR.

'They're not brass,' Marya said.

' 'Brass' is the common name for any metal identification on U.S. Army uniforms.'

'Tradition,' Marya said.

'Tradition,' Peter admitted.

'The word on your lapel must puzzle people who don't know what it stands for,' Marya said.

'Some people think it's a comment,' Peter told her, 'but most don't even notice it.'

'And the eagles on your shoulder?'

'The insignia of a U.S. Army colonel. It shows that the firm thinks I'm as good as a colonel.'

'At least,' Marya agreed. 'And that belt? I've never seen a buckle like that before.'

'War, Inc.'s own design,' Peter said. 'Look, I'll show you a secret.' He gave the front of the buckle a half twist and pulled it off, revealing a compartment within.

'Secret messages?' Marya asked.

'Pills,' Peter said. 'Amphetamine — pep pills — anti-pain pills, and a few others that might be useful. Doctor Steadman is fond of gadgets.' Peter put the front of the buckle back on.

'He must be something of a hypochondriac,' Marya said. 'We're almost at Badabba,' she added, as they bounced by a long line of parked Army trucks.

'It looks like the King wanted to secure the area,' Peter said.

'He didn't want the guerrillas to interfere with his speech,' Marya said, 'but not all the trucks were for soldiers. A lot of them were used to transport farmers to the fair.'

They drove around a last curve, over a final rut, and arrived at a large clearing. Marya parked the jeep by the side of the road, and they got out.

The whole clearing seemed to be filled with booths, religious shrines of various sizes, and people. King Min Lhat was standing on a platform in the middle of the clearing, not quite surrounded by people in ornate robes and be-medaled military uniforms, orating into a microphone. His words were carried to the farthest corner of the huge crowd by a public address system that alternately boomed, echoed and squealed. The speech was in Sadari, but even if it were in English, Peter doubted whether he would have been able to understand it.

'Oh, darn,' Marya said. 'I wanted to get

181

here before the speech started.'

Privately admiring Marya's polite cursing, Peter said, 'Don't worry, I'm sure we can get a copy of the speech that's been mimeographed as a press release.'

'Oh, I know the speech,' Marya said, 'I helped write it. It's just that I wanted to hear my uncle deliver it.'

'That's right,' Peter said, 'the King is your uncle, in a way, isn't he?'

'You may touch me if you like,' Marya told him. 'I may even let you kiss me. After the speech.' She darted into the crowd, headed for the platform.

Not being able to understand the speech, Peter wandered around the edge of the crowd examining the ornate fabric-covered booths holding cages of pigs and piglets, chickens, chicks and other items of farmers' pride both, Peter guessed, for sale and for show. Except for the style of construction of the booths and the hundreds of miniature shrines, it might have been a livestock show in any Iowa town.

'There you are, I've been wanting to talk with you,' a precise voice behind

Peter announced. 'Let's go somewhere we can talk.'

Peter turned around. 'Hello, Logan. What do you need?'

'Come over to the car for a minute, I want to talk to you.'

'Why? I can be insulted here as easily as over by your car.'

'Look, I admit we weren't bosom buddies on first sight, but that's no reason why you can't talk to me for a minute, is it?'

'Talk away, friend. I'll listen.'

Logan sighed. 'Fine,' he said, looking around nervously. 'I'm just trying to be discreet. Come into the open here, away from that tent, and we can talk privately.'

'I'll go along with you that far,' Peter said. 'Wait a second — what was that?' He pointed to a small flap on the tent that was just closing.

'A nosy native,' Logan said. 'Now maybe you understand why I want to go over to the car.'

'I thought I saw the glint of metal,' Peter said. He ran around to the door of the tent and plunged through. Once

183

inside he had to pause for a moment to allow his eyes to adjust to the dim light. Before he had a chance to move, something clubbed him across the chest, knocking him over backwards. A man tried to rush by him as he fell. Twisting, he was just able to grab hold of the man's leg. He pulled the foot back and sideways, and the man lost his balance, falling heavily on top of Peter.

Peter's assailant aimed a vicious kick at him, but he rolled forward and took the blow in his shoulder. The man spun to his feet, and raced for the tent door. Peter jumped up to try to stop him, dizzily grabbing hold of the man's jacket, but the man pulled free.

'Hold on, there.' Logan was at the door, and he gathered up the man and threw him back inside with one motion. 'What are you up to, my little friend?'

The man tried to rush past Logan again, but Logan took his arm, twisted him around, forced him to the ground and sat on him. 'Listening at tent-holes, eh?'

'More than that,' Peter said. 'He hit me

with something when I came in here, and I think . . . ' He looked around the corners of the tent. 'Yes, here it is.'

'A rifle!' Logan said, as Peter retrieved the object.

'He seemed to think it was a baseball bat. But he was using it as a rifle when I saw the barrel sticking out of that flap.' Peter lifted the small square of canvas. 'A well-placed hole it is, too,' he said, looking out. 'It gives an excellent view of the platform.'

'An assassin,' Logan said. He lifted the little man up by the lapels of his jacket. 'Is that what you are — an assassin?' The man just stared at him, and made no reply. 'What should we do with him?' Logan demanded.

'Turn him over to the police, I suppose — or the Army.'

'Right,' Logan agreed. 'Both at once. There were several MPs wandering around here before, let's make them a present of him.' They took their prisoner out of the tent and turned him over to a pair of military policemen who were standing on the outskirts of the crowd.

The corporal in charge promised to take good care of him.

'We're heroes,' Logan said, as they made their way back to the tent.

'So it would seem,' Peter agreed.

On the platform, King Min Lhat paused in his speech, and the crowd broke into wild applause at whatever he had just said. During the pause, while the King waited for the cheering to stop, an MP ran over to the platform and whispered something to one of the officers, who leaned forward and relayed it to the King. He nodded gravely, and continued to speak.

'There's a brave man,' Peter said, indicating the King.

'I suppose,' Logan said, 'although the assassin was probably trying for the Prime Minister. Here, we can talk here.'

'Fine,' Peter agreed, stopping with Logan in front of the tent.

'I've been checking on you,' Logan told him, 'and you're all right.'

'That's nice,' Peter said. 'Checking what?'

'I'm,' Logan said, glancing around to

make sure they were alone, 'a field agent for the CIA.'

'Really?'

'Yes. Of course I don't carry credentials, but you can check with the embassy if you don't believe me.'

'I'll take your word for it,' Peter said.

'That's good,' Logan said, sounding somehow disappointed. 'I had your record checked.'

'Why?' Peter asked.

'You were a major in Army Intelligence before you went to work for this outfit, and the people you worked for thought very highly of you.'

'They lie, or they have short memories,' Peter said. 'They thought I was too independent and reacted badly to discipline. Why did you have my record checked?'

'You're a loyal American citizen,' Logan told Peter.

'It sounds like you want something,' Peter said. 'You'd better tell me what it is.'

'Your help,' Logan said.

'In doing what?'

'We,' Logan announced, 'want to help the people of this country.'

'That's what I'm here for,' Peter said.

'Yes, well, basically we approve of your policies.'

Peter said, 'That's nice of you,' and smiled encouragingly.

'I mean,' Logan went on, 'we realize that if War, Inc., was merely an arm of the United States government, you'd lose a lot of your flexibility.'

'And a lot of customers,' Peter added.

'What's that?'

'If Weapons Analysis and Research was just offering its own version of American military policy, our customers could get what they want from the Pentagon a hell of a lot cheaper than we could give it to them.'

'I suppose,' Logan said, 'but, in this case, that isn't the question. There's no real difference in policy between what we want and what you're trying to do.'

Peter sat down and rubbed his shoulder.

'Does it still hurt?' Logan asked sympathetically.

'Smarts a bit,' Peter admitted. 'Tell me more about this congruity of interests you say we have with the CIA.'

'We're both after the same thing in Bonterre,' Logan said, orating in a low voice. 'The elimination of Communism, and the creation of a stable government where Communism won't be able to flourish.'

'Perhaps our definitions are different,' Peter suggested.

Logan didn't hear, or chose to ignore the comment. 'The face of world Communism is stable in Europe, and the emerging African nations have gradually been turning away from the pie-in-the-sky blandishments of the Kremlin and Peking. The major efforts of both camps of the Communist world are centered today in Asia. It's therefore necessary for the United States and the rest of the Free World to resist this push, not to bring other nations into our power block, but to uphold their right to self-determination.' Logan paused for breath.

'You sound like a right-wing editorial,' Peter said.

'You don't agree?'

'You've dangerously over-simplified a very complex problem. There are more crayons available for use in the coloring book than black and white. Besides, you have more in mind than giving me a lecture on the evils of Communism. I agree with you, to continue on the third-grade level, that Communism is bad and Democracy is good. Now, get to the point.'

At that moment a loud cheer broke out from the assembled crowd. Peter and Logan looked over to the platform. King Lhat, having just finished his speech, bathed in the applause and then sat down. The Prime Minister got up to fill the void. More loud cheering greeted him as he stepped before the microphone. *'Ferthu Theoden hal . . . '* his trained voice took up where the King had left off.

Logan turned back to Peter. 'It's a more complex problem, you're right. In a sense, that is my point. What you and your group are doing here is training the Army to drive off the Communist guerrillas. But that isn't enough. Unless a stable government exists, the Communists will win by default what they're unable to win by open battle. And the present government of Bonterre is anything but stable.'

'It seems pretty stable to me,' said Peter. 'It's the same type of democracy that we've practiced for close to two hundred years in the United States with fair success.'

Logan pounded his fist against his open hand for emphasis. 'The situation's different, can't you see that? The colonists in America were ready for democracy, they were a literate, articulate group, interested in the problems of self-government. The natives here aren't ready for the ballot yet — they'll vote for whoever promises them the most.'

'Have you been following the pattern of elections in the United States?' Peter asked.

'You know what I mean,' Logan said. 'Stop trying to be funny.'

'Sorry about that.'

'These people are children,' Logan insisted.

'What does daddy have in mind for them?' asked Peter.

'Not daddy,' Logan said, 'more like big brother.'

'That's a particularly unfortunate image,'

Peter told him. 'I don't mean to keep sounding so belligerent, but if you'd stop feeding me all this hash and get down to the solid meat, we might get somewhere. I've obviously heard all this before, from both sides, and already have my own opinions on the subject. If you'll tell me what you want from me, I'll tell you what I think of the idea, and maybe we can get down to business.'

Logan decided to be blunt. 'This is off the record,' he said. 'If you try to quote me, I'll deny it, of course. The classification of what I'm about to tell you is Top Secret. We can't hold you to it, since you're not in the Army any more, but if you do divulge it, we can make it rough for you. I hold you to your honor to respect the classification of this information whether you agree to help or not.'

A threat and an appeal to honor in the same breath, Peter reflected, *this must be quite something*. 'Go on,' he said.

Logan took this as agreement with his cautioning. 'There is a movement here to overthrow the government of Bonterre,' he told Peter.

'I know that,' said Peter.

'I mean, aside from the guerrillas,' Logan amended.

'That's right. The so-called 'rightist' group.'

'What do you know about them?' Logan asked.

Peter grinned. 'Only what I read in the papers,' he said.

'What do you mean?'

'I mean that I haven't talked to anyone claiming to represent them. All I know about them is hearsay. They represent many of the old landowners and other established-interest groups. They're just about as strongly against the present democratic government as they are against the guerrillas. They're waiting for the two groups to destroy each other so that they can regain control. Beyond that, I can tell you nothing whatever about them.'

'You've got the general idea, but you seem to have a slightly warped viewpoint. They just don't think the government can win against the Communist guerrilla forces. It's not just a matter of popular support, it's also a question of strength and determination, and the present government just doesn't have it.'

'You seem to know a lot about the rightist viewpoint.'

'I've heard,' Logan admitted cautiously. 'As a matter of fact, I've communicated to my superiors my belief that the wisest thing the United States can do is to support this group. They have the will to win, and they'd form the strongest base for an anti-Communist government possible in Bonterre.'

'Do you think they have the support of the people?' Peter asked.

Logan snorted. 'Give them an efficient propaganda setup, and in two months they'd have the people eating out of their hands.'

'What about land reform, and all that sort of thing?'

'Why should a government have the right to take land away from the people who own it to give it to a lot of peasants who wouldn't know what to do with it?' Logan asked. 'It's one of the things the Communists keep promising to do when they're trying to take over a country, but are smart enough not to try when they have control.'

'That may be,' Peter said, 'but the present government of Bonterre has set up a program to do just that. In fact, I had understood that that's one of the things the rightists are up in arms about.'

'Look,' Logan said, getting chummy, 'wouldn't you get pissed off if somebody started giving away your property?'

'I suppose,' Peter admitted. 'What's the point of all this?'

'We want your help,' Logan said.

'We who? And help doing what?'

'We, CIA; and help in assisting the rightist group regain power.'

What that means is me, CIA's little old local representative, I'll bet, Peter thought.

'What sort of help?' he asked.

'The rightists are planning a coup to take control of the government, and we could use the assistance of your people in keeping it bloodless.'

'In other words, aside from any other consideration, you want me to help double-cross the government who hired us, is that right?'

'I'm sure the new government would keep you on,' Logan told him.

'Sure, but how many other jobs would we get if word of anything like this got out?'

'Word would never get out,' Logan insisted.

'Sorry, can't help you,' Peter said, standing up and dusting off his pants.

'I was hoping to get your willing support, Mister Carthage,' Logan said.

'I'm sorry to disappoint you, then. You should never count your chickens, and like that.'

'I was hoping I wouldn't have to do this,' Logan said with the air of a man who was about to pull the fifth ace out of his sleeve.

'Do what?' asked Peter.

'Mister Carthage, it's the considered opinion of some people in the American government that you might be in considerable danger of losing your American citizenship. Now, with my help, that might be avoided.'

'Go over that again,' Peter demanded, 'slowly.'

'You're in the employ of the armed forces of a foreign government. According to the Constitution of the United States, that's one of the things that citizenship can be revoked for.'

'The preposition is a part of speech you're not supposed to end a sentence with,' said Peter, 'but let it pass. I suggest you read the relevant passages of the Constitution again, and then you can come see me and apologize. Thanks for the offer, sorry I can't take you up on it. It's been fun talking to you, see you around.' Leaving Logan sputtering in the middle distance, Peter continued his tour of the fair grounds.

After a while the speeches were over, and the King's sandals were auctioned off. Peter sought out Marya.

'I heard about what you did,' she told him.

'Oh,' he said. 'Well, don't believe a word of it. You should never listen to stories like that.'

'I think it was wonderful,' Marya said, taking Peter's hand. 'You saved my uncle's life and captured the assassin. We heard all about it.'

'Oh, that.'

'My uncle wanted to thank you himself, but his advisors said that it would be better not to draw attention to the assassination attempt, so he said I could thank you for him.' She reached up, put her arms around his neck, and kissed him enthusiastically on the lips. 'Thank you.'

'The nicest thank you a man could ask for,' Peter told her.

'Come on.' Marya pulled him toward the jeep. 'I'll drive you back to town, and we'll have dinner together.' Peter allowed himself to be pulled.

As Marya bounced the jeep happily back to town, Peter mentally went over the conversation he had had with Logan. The threat to himself was nonsense, he reflected, but just how serious was the threat to the government of Bonterre?

Peter doubted that Logan was acting with the full knowledge of the American government. He had all the earmarks of a man dedicated to a set of beliefs, and would probably have colored his reports in favor of those beliefs. There should be something that could be done to bring the information Logan was sending in back to perspective, the trick was to find out what that something was.

Peter decided to have a talk with the American ambassador to Bonterre as soon as possible, and find out what his views on the situation were. Peter had met the ambassador only once, at the palace, as War, Inc.'s policy was to keep away from representatives of any government except the one they were working with; but the policy would have to be stretched in this case.

'You're not listening,' Marya said.

'You're right,' Peter admitted, bringing his attention back to here and now. 'What were you saying?'

'Pineapples,' Marya said.

'Oh?'

'Wild pineapples,' she explained, 'growing along the road. They're even sweeter than the cultivated ones, but not quite so juicy. Here, I'll show you.' She pulled the jeep over to the side of the road and jumped out. 'Follow me, and bring the machete from the back seat.'

Peter slid the heavy, curved blade from its canvas sheath and walked into the woods after Marya.

Marya paused and inspected a thicket. 'Give me the blade,' she said. Peter handed the machete to her. She hacked away with abandon, sending wood, leaves and bamboo flying, then dived into the thicket and hacked some more. 'Here,' she said, coming up with a pineapple. With a few expert strokes of the machete she cut off the top, trimmed the sides and sliced off a piece of the fruit to hand to Peter.

'You're a wicked girl with a machete,' Peter said.

'Years of practice,' she said, smiling. She cut off a piece for herself, and then sat down on the ground to munch on it. Peter sat beside her and bit into the piece she had given him.

'I don't really think you were sufficiently thanked before,' Marya started tentatively.

'What's that?'

'You may kiss me again — if you like,' she explained.

'Oh,' Peter said gravely. 'Thank you.' He leaned forward, took her face in his hands, and kissed her firmly on the lips.

'You're not taking me seriously,' Marya complained. 'That was like an old-friend kiss . . . We don't know each other well enough for that sort of mild, disinterested kissing.'

'What sort do you recommend?' Peter asked, laughing.

'The 'hey — maybe if we get to know each other better we might decide to become lovers' kind of kiss is much more fun with the right person. You don't have a girl friend or anything, do you?' Marya asked, with sudden concern.

'Not even 'or anything,'' Peter assured her.

'That's nice,' she said. 'It goes like this.' She pushed him down to the ground, moistened her lips, closed her eyes and kissed in a passionately experimental manner.

There was a crashing sound in the woods, and Marya raised herself to look. 'Oh, damn,' she whispered, 'talk about bad timing. I think we're in trouble.'

'Your father?' Peter suggested.

'Don't be silly. Guerrillas, I think.'

'That's swell. How many?'

'I saw two, wait a second.' She sat up again, shaking off Peter's attempt to pull her down.

'Keep your head down,' Peter urged quietly.

'I know what I'm doing, don't worry,' she said. 'Three, there's three of them.' She rolled off Peter. 'Okay, man, do your stuff.'

'Your confidence in me is dismaying, but we'll see what we can do.' He took his .38 out of the holster. 'See how quietly you can crawl into that hole you cut in the thicket,' he directed Marya, 'and keep down.'

'Down it is, sir,' she whispered. 'Any time.' Clutching the machete, she wriggled and crawled silently into the thicket, and then smiled and blew Peter a kiss.

Like a knight in a tournament, Peter thought, *I should have her handkerchief tucked into my sleeve.* He directed his attention to the guerrillas, who were sneaking along next to the road. Two of them

202

were armed with submachine guns, and the third had a holstered sidearm. *Must be an officer*, Peter mused, *wonder what they're after?*

The three of them came upon the jeep parked at the side of the road and started an earnest conversation. *They're after us*, Peter realized. *I'd better do something before it occurs to them that the occupants of the jeep are probably very close by. Maybe the antitheft gadget Jurgens put in the jeep can be made to work for us.*

Peter decided that he'd better concentrate on the two with submachine guns first, and waited until they were standing side-by-side at the jeep. *About a hundred yards*, he figured, *should be able to do that with my eyes closed*. He steadied his arm against a rock and, aiming very carefully, squeezed off two shots. Both men went down. *Jurgens would approve*, Peter thought. Before he had time to shoot again, the third guerrilla had dropped, grabbed one of the fallen machine guns, and rolled. *A sharp boy*, Peter decided, *just great!* He held his fire as the guerrilla officer disappeared behind the jeep.

A burst of gunfire came from behind the jeep, and bullets splattered the ground to Peter's left. *He doesn't know where we are*, Peter thought. He turned around to see how Marya was taking it. Flat against the ground in the middle of the thicket, she smiled at him and gave the thumbs-up sign.

A burst of gunfire kicked up dirt right in front of them. Exposing himself as little as possible, Peter aimed the pistol at the jeep, determined to wait until he had a clear shot so as not to give away his position.

His target moved around behind the jeep, but stayed concealed. Then Peter saw a hand reach cautiously up toward the jeep's 'on' switch. *Now!* Peter thought.

The hand clicked the switch. A loud siren went off, and the jeep was enveloped in a cloud of smoke.

Without pausing to think, Peter was up and running toward the jeep. The guerrilla had dropped his submachine gun and was stumbling away from the cloud of tear gas, clawing at his eyes and coughing. Peter dived at him and unceremoniously smashed him across the side of his head with the pistol. The guerrilla collapsed.

Peter sat down on the road and took several deep breaths. Then he thoughtfully removed the Mauser pistol from the guerrilla's holster. When Marya came out of the woods he was busy tying the guerrilla's arms behind him with the man's own belt.

'Very good,' Marya said, 'excellent. I'm proud of you.'

'Any hero would have done the same,' Peter told her. 'I'd better check on the other two.'

'I already did,' Marya told him. 'They're both dead. You're quite a shot.'

Holding his breath, Peter went over to the jeep and shut off the siren. 'We'll get this one back to town as soon as the tear gas clears away,' he said.

12

'Name and rank is all I am required to give,' the guerrilla announced. 'That is according to the regulations of war.' He sat on a small stool in Fort Alpha's interrogation room and stared defiantly at the three men who faced him.

Colonel Lyet leaned forward. 'War?' he asked. 'What war is that? I don't know of any country that Bonterre is at war with.'

'The People's Democracy of Bonterre is at war with your puppet government,' the guerrilla spat.

Tony Ryan stirred in his chair. 'Nasty little brute, isn't he?' he enquired gently.

'We respect no regulations of war against a band of outlaws who murder women and children,' Colonel Lyet said. 'As far as I'm concerned, you're nothing but a criminal, and deserve to be treated no better than a mass murderer.'

The guerrilla lifted up his head. 'Name and rank,' he said. 'You may torture me, but I will tell you nothing else.'

'All right,' Peter said, 'let's start there. What's your name and rank?'

'Captain Thombo Quat, Bonterre People's Volunteer Rebel Army,' the prisoner stated firmly.

'Hi, there, Thombo,' Tony said cheerfully, 'open your yap and talk to us. We want to hear how well you can sing.'

'Sing?' Quat looked startled. 'What is this 'sing'?'

'In your best soprano,' Tony told him. 'We want a song all about the guerrillas. Where they are, what they're doing, all that sort of thing.'

'I will tell you nothing, torture me as you will,' Quat declared, but he looked worried.

Colonel Lyet growled.

'Torture you?' Peter asked. 'Who wants to torture you?'

Quat thought that over for a minute. Now he looked both worried and puzzled. 'You hope to win me over by good treatment?' he asked disdainfully. 'You cannot fool me that way.'

'Just average treatment,' Peter said, 'but

I think you might decide to talk. Let me tell you of the brilliant idea I have for persuading you to wholeheartedly tell us everything you know.'

'It's very nasty,' Tony assured him.

Quat glared at Tony, and said nothing.

'You'll be taken from here,' Peter started, 'to a small, select cell we have waiting for you. There special guards will keep you in isolation. You'll be allowed to speak to no one, except, once a day, one of us will come to visit with you and chat for a while.'

'You will never break me down with solitary confinement,' Quat snapped.

'Of course not,' Peter said soothingly, 'nothing like that. We'll only keep you there for two weeks.'

'And at the end of two weeks, if I haven't talk you'll shoot me?'

'It's an idea,' Colonel Lyet said sharply. 'It's what you'd do.'

'You have a nasty and suspicious mind,' Peter told the prisoner. 'If you haven't talked inside of the two weeks, we'll decide that you're a brave and honorable opponent, and let you go.'

'What?' Quat sat up straight. 'What sort of trick . . .'

'A very nasty one,' said Tony, 'we're quite proud of it.'

'At the end of two weeks,' Peter continued, 'there will be a little formality before we release you. We'll take you, under guard, to a special suite in one of Bonterre's most luxurious hotels. After you've been there about a week, we'll arrange for you to have a 'secret' audience with the King, who will present you with a medal. Then we'll take you back to the hotel and allow you to escape. You can then trot right back to your comrades in the jungle.'

'Knowing what you've been doing through their agents in the city,' Tony added, 'they'll doubtless be overjoyed to see you and welcome you back in their ranks. No?'

'They might even all ask to see the medal,' Peter suggested. 'Think it over, we'll be talking to you.' The three of them got up.

Captain Quat looked even more worried as they left the room.

It was graduation day at Fort Alpha. The first class of Bonterre's new Special Forces had completed the six-week training course, and were now engaged in the age-old military tradition of marching in review past a specially erected grandstand. The personnel of War, Inc., were on the grandstand, along with King Min, the Prime Minister, lesser government officials, and every general of the Bonterre Army that was in the capital at the time. General Motyse, commander in chief of the Army and an old-line rightist, was standing alongside of the King trying not to show his distaste for the whole procedure. His subordinates were ranged below him with carefully impassive faces.

A new class would graduate from Fort Alpha's school once every two weeks from now on, but this was the first, the test class that would either prove or disprove the value of War, Inc.'s training. Interest ran high.

The equipment ordered for the new Special Forces units had finally arrived in sufficient quantity as to be used for more than training purposes, and some of it — that which would be used to outfit the first company — was being displayed. Several German DO 32 one-man observation helicopters whirled slowly by in front of the marching men, and two massive Sikorsky troop-carrying helicopters followed the marchers, keeping carefully in line and six feet off the ground. The craft were now piloted by War, Inc., technicians, but would be manned by Bonterre Army pilots as soon as they completed an accelerated training program.

Behind the helicopters came a row of jeeps with recoilless 105mm rifles, and behind the jeeps a line of light tanks. The tanks were part of the base defense, and were just included to make the ceremony more impressive.

'A good group,' Jurgens commented from his spot next to Peter on the grandstand, as the graduating class marched by with their brand new Armalite rifles slung across their backs.

'They march well,' Peter admitted.

'They could do that when they got here,' Jurgens said, 'now they can do a lot more.'

'We hope so,' Peter said. He turned his attention back to the marchers, who had passed the grandstand once, and were now coming back. This time they halted in front of the grandstand and did a right face. Then the speeches started. The King spoke, the Prime Minister added a few words, and then one of the generals expanded on the theme. Jurgens, as chief instructor, was last to speak.

'You've done well,' Jurgens told the class. 'You're all a credit to your profession and your country.' The big Swede paused and looked over the men. 'One thought,' he said. 'You are the future commanders of the Army of Bonterre. Don't ever allow the military to get involved in politics. The government is in the hands of the people, and the Army is in the hands of the government. This is how it should be; always let it remain this way.' He stepped down.

Colonel Lyet, who had been put in command of the First Special Forces Battalion, made up of graduates of the

Fort Alpha school, stepped in front of the men. He saluted the King, and then did a snappy about face. 'Dismissed,' he barked.

The men cheered, tossed their Special Forces berets into the air, and then broke ranks. The ceremony was officially over.

That evening, after dinner, the War, Inc., command group, with Trimam and Colonel Lyet as unofficial observers, gathered for their weekly discussion and progress report. Professor Perlemutter started the proceedings by opening an imposing looking attaché case he was carrying, and producing two folders and a bottle of brandy. After the brandy was properly decanted and distributed, the good professor started on the folders.

'I have here,' he said, picking up one of the folders and weighing it in his hand, 'the file of reports from my private agents. I wish I could be more definite about this. I'd like to be able to give you time and date along with precise plan of action, but all I can affirm is that the event will happen. Gentlemen, within the next month the rightist coup that Mister Logan so nicely warned us about is scheduled to take place.'

'You're sure of this?' Colonel Lyet asked sharply.

'I'm not privy to the minutes of the meetings of the leaders of the group, but my sources of information are reliable as far as they go. An interesting sidelight on the thinking of these people, they've decided to keep War, Inc., on to help them get rid of the guerrillas after they take power.'

Trimam asked Peter, 'Would you stay if the government fell?'

'In this particular case,' Peter answered, 'we'll do everything we can to prevent that from happening. Although just what we can do remains to be seen. We don't know what they're planning yet.'

'I'll keep my, er, ears opened, and see what else I can find out,' Perlemutter said, 'but I'm not too hopeful. The members of the group that are known to us, like General Motyse, for example, are very careful not to do anything that might give us a lead. There seems to be a secret head of the organization that coordinates the planning, and I can't find out who it is. Oh, incidentally,' he waggled a finger at Bob Alvin, 'this brash young man and his computing machines have been of great aid to me in another project that has just reached fruition. I've obtained copies of all the messages Mister Logan has sent through the telegraph office since his arrival here, and with the aid of young Alvin, I've solved the cipher system he's using. We've just finished writing a program for the computer to decipher the stuff as fast as we can type it into the machine.'

'What does the bastard have to say for himself?' Jurgens demanded.

'Ask me in a few days,' Perlemutter said. 'We just finished writing the program this afternoon, so we haven't got much of it broken out yet. But, from now on we'll be able to read his stuff as fast as he sends it out — for whatever that's worth.' He sat down.

'What other business?' Peter asked.

'The raid,' Jurgens said, 'all set for tomorrow?'

'Right,' Peter told him. 'Ready to go ahead as planned.'

'What raid?' Ambassador Trimam asked.

'We got information from our prize prisoner about the location of the guerrilla base in this area, so we've planned a surprise strike,' Peter explained.

'So,' Trimam said, 'your diabolical plan worked.'

'Yes, indeed. He decided he was more afraid of his own men than of us if we did what we threatened. He thought it was quite unfair, but he talked.'

'Are you going on this raid?' Perlemutter asked.

'Of course Jurgens and I are going,' Peter said.

'May I remind you of the pertinent paragraph in our manual?'

'What's that?'

'War, Inc., personnel are to avoid situations that involve actual battle contact with enemy troops, and are to engage in only training exercises . . . '

'Ya — so?' Jurgens interrupted. 'This is a training exercise, just like it says in the book. I always follow what the book says.'

'Of course,' Perlemutter agreed, seeing that he was outgunned, 'how silly of me.'

★　★　★

At five-twenty the next morning Peter walked into the mess hall and joined Jurgens at the instructors' table in one corner. The new graduates of Bonterre Special Forces' Strategic Assault Unit One were eating quietly at the other tables.

'Green light,' Peter said, setting his tray across from Jurgens. 'Everything's ready for this morning's main event.'

'Excellent,' Jurgens said, sliding a poached egg into his mouth. 'And the supporting infantry?'

'Last night Foxtrot and Golf companies of the Third Battalion entered the Quantor Valley area around Bon Ville on routine maneuvers, and settled down for the night. In about half an hour they will receive orders to seal off the area and coordinate with our assault.'

'Fine,' Jurgens approved. 'Now if the guerrillas' intelligence network hasn't picked this up, it should be an interesting morning.'

'Let's hope,' Peter said, and started in

on his own eggs.

Forty minutes later Peter and Jurgens watched as Colonel Lyet completed the final inspection of the combat-ready troops. When he was satisfied, he dismissed them, and the men boarded the waiting helicopters for their first ride into combat.

'The hunters are about to become the hunted,' Lyet said to Peter and Jurgens as they joined him, 'and it's about goddam time.'

'That's one thing about this new style of fighting that I can't get used to,' Jurgens said. 'Combat for one or two days, and then back to camp. No line holding or fighting for ground.'

'A new type of football,' Peter agreed. 'But that's the way they play it, so that's the way we'll play it. The object is to destroy the enemy's force and his will to fight, not to get land. Whoever wins the war gets control of the whole country anyhow.'

'Well,' said Colonel Lyet, 'let's see how many of these new tricks the old dog's been able to learn. Shall we, gentlemen?'

He gestured toward the helicopters.

'Right,' said Peter. The three men walked across the field in the pre-dawn light, and climbed on board the waiting copters, one of them in each machine. The pilot of Peter's copter gave him the thumbs-up sign as he clambered aboard.

It was drizzling, and a mist hung low over the jungle as the three copters approached the target area, a clearing about a quarter of a mile away from the suspected guerrilla stronghold. Peter, holding a machine rifle and leaning against the web belt fastened across the open door of the middle copter, watched the green blur of treetops passing below him. The overhanging foliage could have concealed divisions of troops, or even a lost civilization, from the view of anyone passing overhead.

'Make ready, please,' the pilot's voice sounded loud over the intercom. The men crowded into the copter stood up and flexed their knees to remove the stiffness of sitting. Peter grabbed a hand hold by the door, and unfastened the belt. The clearing came into view, and seconds later the copter had settled lightly to the ground.

'Goodbye,' the pilot said distinctly. Peter jumped the foot and a half to the ground, and moved forward to give the men behind him room. As soon as all of the men were out of the copter, it lifted and disappeared into the mist.

The two squad leaders from Peter's copter formed their men around them. The ground was muddy, and made walking difficult. It looked like a scene from a silent movie, as the men walked with an exaggerated motion, lifting then-feet high to clear the mud. The steady drizzle falling against the leaves made a background noise that blanked out the sounds made by the men.

At a hand signal from Colonel Lyet, the six squad leaders started their squads into the jungle. Peter walked along with, but slightly separate from, the fourth squad. He was there essentially as an observer to see how well these men performed, and he didn't want any of the squad leaders relying on him when they should be using their own judgment.

The jungle closed in around them almost immediately, and the squads lost sight of each other. The squad radioman stayed up front with the squad leader, listening for any word from Colonel Lyet, who would be the first to break radio silence.

For fifteen minutes the men worked their way deeper into the jungle. Then the men came up to their point scout, who stood beside a tree waiting for them to catch up. After a brief, whispered talk with the scout, the squad leader sent runners to the right and left, and beckoned for Peter to come forward.

'What is it?' Peter asked softly.

'Possibly a stroke of luck,' the squad leader told him. 'Over to the left about five yards we intersect what would seem to be a well-used trail.'

Colonel Lyet came stamping through the mud to examine the trail. 'Very good,' he said after a few minutes. 'It would appear to be a supply route. They've probably got it guarded where it enters their camp, but I doubt if they're expecting any trouble. Have you got two men who can quietly take out a couple of guards?'

'Yes, sir,' the squad leader said positively.

'Send them on ahead. Give them two minutes, then follow. I'll send the third squad along behind you. Pick off the guards first, but wait for word that I'm in position before you go in.'

'Yes, sir.'

'So,' Colonel Lyet said. He turned and disappeared back into the jungle.

The squad leader called two men to him and gave them instructions. They nodded, handed their rifles to other men in the squad, unsheathed the wicked-looking Fairbairn commando knives, and went silently up the trail.

Two minutes later the rest of the squad fell in and started up the trail. The third squad joined the tail of the fourth.

The travel went a lot faster along the thin trail. It was only a short time later when the squad leader halted the column. 'Through there,' he whispered to Peter, pointing into the trees.

13

Peter looked, but could see nothing but trees. 'I'll take your word for it,' he said. 'Did your men get the guards?'

'There was only one guard — he's been taken care of.' The squad leader's matter-of-factness, Peter decided, concealed a bloodthirsty soul.

'Sir,' the radioman whispered, 'we are to attack in one minute, at the colonel's signal.'

The squad leader raised his hand, and the two squads of men prepared to charge.

There had been a lot of discussion the night before about whether the attack should be made as noisily or as quietly as possible. The quiet faction had won; the reasoning being that yelling, while it might confuse the enemy, would also alert him. A silent attack might make him wonder what was going on while he should have been reaching for his rifle.

'Now,' the colonel's voice sounded over the walkie-talkie. 'Now,' the radioman whispered to the squad leader. The squad leader dropped his hand.

Guns at ready, the third and fourth squad walked around the last curve in the trail. At this point the trail broadened to something like a street, and three long buildings went back into the jungle from each side. From the wooden-frame construction of the buildings, and from the badly weathered markings on the nearest one, Peter decided that at one time the long-gone French Army had made use of the buildings for some sort of supply depot.

There were four men in the street when the attack force came into view. Three of the men froze, but the fourth tried to reach for a rifle slung around his neck.

A burst of machine-gun fire echoed hollowly down the street. The man reaching for his gun clutched his side and fell into the mud. One of the other men toppled over slowly, with a 'there's been some mistake' look on his face. Of the two remaining men, one dropped to the street and rolled toward a building, the other made a dash for the doorway. The rolling man made it, the other was cut down before he got three steps.

Answering fire started coming from the windows of the buildings, and the two squads took cover and started working their way forward.

Peter ducked behind a log, aimed at the nearest window and started squeezing off shots. Someone was firing from inside the window, but he was either aiming at another target or he was a lousy shot. Still, Peter kept his head down.

Noises came from the two sides of the compound, showing that the rest of Colonel Lyet's small army had joined the attack.

A sharp ping sounded close to Peter's head. Peter's target had spotted him. Peter ducked and tried to move out; but every time he showed his head someone shot at it from the window.

Peter let off a burst of shots at the window, which made the defender drop out of sight. *He'll be back up in a second*, Peter reasoned, sighting in carefully, *and his first shot'll be low. He'll be aiming for where he thinks I jumped to when I got his head down.*

The sniper reappeared, and Peter fired. At the same instant a slug tore into the wood three inches below his head. The man in the window jerked back, out of sight. *I was wrong*, Peter decided, *but he missed, and I don't think I did*. He waited a second, then ran in a low crouch over to the window.

Taking a grenade from his belt, he pulled the pin and tossed it through the window. There was a crump, the earth shook slightly, and a shower of glass and debris came through the window. Peter stood up and looked through the window into what was left of the room. Two men lay in the grotesque positions of violent death in what had once been an office.

Peter climbed gingerly through the window and looked around the room. It was sparsely furnished, and the only object of interest was a large metal filing cabinet that had probably been left behind by the French. It was opened, with papers scattered around, and the corpse by the door had a large pile of papers at his side. It looked as if he had been trying to salvage them when the grenade went off.

Peter made a mental note to have the papers carefully examined, then went to the door. The outside corridor was empty. Holding his rifle ready, he stepped out into the corridor. Nothing happened. He went up to the next door, which was open, and cautiously peered into the room. It was empty. Peter found the next four rooms also deserted.

At the door to the fifth room he heard a noise — a curiously muted scraping sound — from inside. He tried the handle, and pushed the door open. On the other side of the room there was an open trapdoor in the floor. Two men, one halfway down into the trap and the other standing above it, whirled around as he came in. They were both in the uniforms of high-ranking officers in the guerrilla force.

'Hold it!' Peter barked, hoping to shock the men into inactivity by his sudden appearance.

The standing man dropped and fired the machine gun he was holding in one motion that was so smooth that he must have stayed up nights practicing it. His bullets and the ones from Peter's gun passed in the air.

Peter felt a hot pain in the right side of his chest, and a curious numbness in his right arm. His machine gun fell to the floor. *This will never do*, Peter thought, and bent over to retrieve the gun. He started to fall forward, and didn't know it when he hit the floor.

14

Awareness returned to him slowly: first cold, then pain, and then a sense of orientation. The cold permeated his body. The pain was concentrated on his right side. The orientation: he was lying on his back in a sort of cocoon that opened at the top. There was no sense of time, and reality and fantasy intermingled. He would almost regain consciousness, and then slip back into dreams. The dreams were all unpleasant.

He almost awoke one time when something was drilling into his chest on the painful right side. He may have screamed, but then he passed out again.

A sharp pain — a brand new sharp pain — in his left foot. He woke up screaming.

'That will do,' a voice said. The pain lessened.

'Mister Carthage! Wake up, Mister Carthage!' His face was slapped several times. He groaned and opened his eyes.

Focus. Someone was leaning over him. Focus. The cocoon-like thing enveloping him was a hammock; he was in a room of some sort in a wooden-frame building. The man leaning over him was in the surprisingly ornate uniform of a guerrilla general.

'Can you hear me, Mister Carthage?'

'Uh.' He tried to say something, but the words wouldn't form. Again the general slapped him sharply across the face.

'Hey!' He tried to move his face out of the way. 'Cut it out.'

'Good,' the figure bending over him said, 'you're awake. I will give you a minute, and then we'll talk.' The face receded from view.

Peter tried to sort out the sensations. The pain: he remembered being shot, it was the last thing he did remember. He wondered how many bullets he had picked up. It couldn't have been too many, he decided, or he wouldn't be here. He wondered where 'here' was.

The cold: he must have a chill, fever induced by shock and loss of blood. He was shivering, and felt as if he had just taken a long sleep in an ice box.

His left foot hurt. It seemed unlikely, and then he remembered that that was how they had woken him up. *They must*, he decided, *want me to talk while I'm still alive.* The thought didn't cheer him up.

'We'll talk now, Mister Carthage,' the general said from the other side of the room. Someone tipped the hammock, and two pair of hands grabbed him as he fell out. A surge of dizziness hit him as he was pulled upright. He was half tugged and half carried across the room, and sat on a wooden stool. Everything started to blur, and he fell sideways off the stool. It seemed to take a long time.

Hands grabbed his hair and jerked him sharply upright into a sitting position. This new, sharp pain cut through the dizziness. He was suddenly wide awake, and racked by waves of nausea.

'What can you tell us, Mister Carthage?' the general asked, standing above him and staring down.

'I'm going to be sick,' Peter said. Convulsively, he threw up.

'*Merde!*' The general stepped quickly back. 'All over my boots.'

Someone slapped Peter across the top of his head, which made him gag but didn't stop the nausea.

'Leave him alone,' the general said. 'When he's done, clean up the mess and call me.' He left the room.

A few minutes later Peter was entirely done. He felt as if he'd been purged of most of his insides. As the nausea subsided, weakness and dizziness took over again. He slumped forward on the stool, but was careful not to fall off. The rough hands, with some equally rough cloth, cleaned up his face and uniform a bit and mopped up the floor around him.

The general came back into the room. 'Now we can talk,' he suggested.

'Sure,' Peter agreed. He stared at the floor, both hands gripping the sides of the stool to keep himself upright on it.

'Look at me,' the general suggested pleasantly, jerking Peter's head up. Peter's stomach heaved, and for a second he looked as if he were going to throw up again. The general hurriedly let go.

Doesn't like puke, Peter thought. *That's probably funny.*

The general snapped his fingers, and somebody brought him a chair, which was set down directly opposite Peter's stool. The general lowered himself into the chair. 'I am Lin Tsui, Commanding General of the People's Army. You are Peter Carthage, head of the American imperialist training mission to the fascist Bonterre Government. So?'

'A truly objective presentation of the facts,' Peter said.

General Tsui swung. The backhand caught Peter full on the side of the face and knocked him from the stool. He could taste blood in his mouth, and feel it drip down the side of his face. The hands lifted him back on to the stool.

'There are some things I'd like you to tell me,' the general went on, as if nothing had happened. 'I think we will have a long talk together. You will talk, yes?'

'What do you want to know?' Peter asked, shaking his head to try to clear the buzzing from his ears.

'Tell me about the attack today,' the

general demanded. 'How did you know the location of our base?'

'Was it supposed to be a secret?' Peter asked.

The general restrained himself with a deliberate effort. 'Two things puzzle us,' he continued, 'and they are possibly related. One is your knowledge of the location of our base, and the other is the fact that we weren't warned of the attack. I will consolidate them into one question: what do you know of X?'

Peter looked up, 'Of what?'

General Tsui stood up. 'There are a group of people in Bonterre who have been aiding the People's Army, without being in sympathy with its goals. They are, as you say in English, playing one end against the other. They supply us with . . . ' he shrugged ' . . . various small items that prove useful, and also with information. It's a sort of barter system, and we pay them well for this service.

'We are aware that there will come a time when they will judge it no longer expedient to continue this service. They will switch sides without warning, and do

234

their best to destroy us. They will not succeed, as a properly founded partisan movement is an irresistible force; but we wish to know when this change of heart takes place.

'The two facts I mentioned — your knowledge of the location of our base and the failure of X to notify us of the attack — would seem to indicate that it has taken place.' He leaned over and asked, 'Is this so?' softly, his face a few inches above Peter's.

'Who is this 'X'?' Peter asked. The thought occurred to him that General Tsui was being so liberal with information because he thought that Peter would never be able to pass it on to anyone.

'Our contact with this group we know only as X. They've been very careful about that. It's of no importance. The question is, have they started to give you information, and if so, how much?'

'What sort of barter is it?' Peter asked. 'What do you give them?'

'Opium,' General Tsui said. 'Now you answer.'

The reply startled Peter. He knew the

general's mysterious 'X' represented the rightists, but he hadn't known they were collecting opium. 'If you had some of it distilled to morphine,' he said, touching the rude bandage around his shoulder, 'I could use it.'

'So sorry,' General Tsui said. 'X turns it into heroin, I understand, but we have none of that here.'

He's giving me more information than I'm giving him, Peter thought. He wondered if he'd ever be able to use it, then decided not to think about that. 'I see. I'm sorry, but I can't tell you a thing about this 'X.' We've never dealt with him.'

'I'm willing to believe you,' General Tsui said. 'Tell me how you got your information, and why we weren't warned of the raid.'

'I can't do that,' Peter answered.

General Tsui hit him again. Again he fell off the stool and was pulled back onto it. 'I'm afraid you don't realize your position,' the general said.

'I think I do,' said Peter. 'I'd like to help you, but I can't. Sorry about that.'

'We'll see,' the general said. He gestured to the two men standing behind Peter. 'You'll find my methods crude, but effective. Very soon you won't be able to think of anything more pleasant than telling me what I want to know.'

A hand twined in Peter's hair, pulling him upright. Another dug into his unbelievably tender right shoulder. Peter gasped.

'You'll find that words will relieve the pressure,' the general told him.

'I'm fresh out,' Peter said between his teeth.

The general nodded. The hand increased its pressure. Peter screamed, and then blanked out. He slid off the stool.

When Peter woke up again, it was dark. He was lying in the mud, and his right side was causing him unbelievable pain. He twisted over onto his back, and lay still. He could see specks of light above him. It took a long time for his eyes to focus well enough for him to decide they were stars.

There was a constant sloshing sound. It was caused, Peter discovered, staring into the dark until his eyes burned, by a guard who was making an erratic circle around where Peter lay. A few minutes later Peter discovered that the circle was bounded by a barbed-wire fence enclosure.

Peter was lying half in and half out of what looked like a poorly made dog house in the middle of a small compound. He seemed to be the only person inside the compound. The first prisoner in stalag number one.

Doctrine has it that the best time to escape is the first chance you have. No matter how hopeless it looks, the odds will get even worse the longer you wait. Peter decided that this was the first chance, and might well be the last. Making as little noise as possible, he released the catch on his belt buckle. He fumbled for the pills inside, recognizing the ones he wanted by shape. Pain killers and amphetamine pep pills. He closed the buckle and chewed thoughtfully on the pills. They were very bitter, but somehow reassuring. At least he was doing something.

A half-hour later the pain was reduced to a dull numbness, and the stimulant pills were making him feel feverishly alert. He couldn't help wondering what price his already weakened system would have to pay for the chemical alertness.

He lay silently for another fifteen minutes until the guard was changed. Now, he decided. As soon as the new guard had passed him on his circuit of the compound, Peter rolled over to the fence and inspected it. It was about eight feet high, with strands of barbed wire every six inches. The fence posts were some four feet apart. The makers of the fence, Peter decided, must have an almost superstitious belief in the effectiveness of barbed wire. He rolled back to the dog house and probed around inside it for a loose stick. After a short search, he found one that was ideal for his purposes: an eighteen-inch-long section of one-by-three board.

Waiting until the guard had again passed him, Peter rolled back over to the fence and used the board to push up the lowest strand of barbed wire until all the slack was out of it. This raised it about a foot off the mud. Peter carefully wriggled through the enlarged hole, and then removed the stick. The barbed wire snapped back into place with a twanging sound. Peter froze, but the guard, who apparently had heard nothing, continued his steady sloshing pace around the compound.

Peter rolled about six feet out, until he was hidden in the middle of a growth of swamp grass, and then waited. When the guard passed, he rose silently out of the grass. Two steps, and he was behind the guard. He crooked his left arm around the guard's neck, and brought his right arm up to complete the strangling lock. The right arm was too weak to complete the motion, and a sharp pain went through Peter's shoulder.

The guard twisted free and brought his rifle butt down in a clubbing motion. Peter sidestepped, caught his foot around the guard's leg, and pushed with his good left arm.

The guard went down, and Peter stamped savagely with the heel of his bare foot, catching the guard in the neck. The guard was still.

Peter picked up the guard's rifle, and

then realized that he could never manage it with one hand. He unfastened the bayonet, stuck it in his belt and started walking.

It was a dark night, and the jungle was thick. After a short time his feet were bleeding and every step was an effort, but he dared not stop. When the effects of the pills wore off he would probably collapse, and he wanted to be as far away as possible from the guerrilla camp when that happened. He plunged blindly through the jungle, tripping over vines and running headlong into tree branches. It was impossible to set a steady pace; where the jungle was thin he stumbled along, where it was thick he had to push his way through. Several times he had to use the bayonet to cut his way through tangled underbrush.

After what seemed to be several hours he came to a trail of sorts. There was a strong possibility that it came from the guerrilla camp, but Peter decided that the increased speed made up for that hazard. He set a fast walking pace, stopping only when he lost the trail and had to take time to find it again.

The dawn came suddenly, as it has a habit of doing in jungles, and with its arrival the last reserve of Peter's energy fled. His walk slowed to a hobble. By sheer will power he kept going for another half hour, and then he dropped. Feet ripped and bleeding, clothes tattered, and with blood oozing slowly from beneath the bandage around his shoulder, he was found two hours later.

15

Marya sat on the little wooden bench and refused to cry. 'You're sure he isn't dead?' she asked.

Jurgens would have liked to comfort the girl in some way, but it's hard to wipe tears away when she refuses to cry. He just stood there. 'We're not sure of anything. He wasn't dead when the guerrillas took him away, or they wouldn't have bothered. All we can do is wait.'

'But you said he was wounded,' the girl insisted.

Jurgens nodded. 'We found his weapon on the floor with blood around it in the room leading to the escape tunnel. That's how the guerrilla high brass escaped, and they took Peter with them.'

'What chance does he have?'

'There's no way of knowing, but Peter's very resourceful.' Jurgens cleared his throat. 'I — er — didn't know that you and Carthage had anything — that is . . . ' He paused awkwardly.

'We didn't,' Marya told him, 'but we might have. Somehow that's worse.' Jurgens nodded as if he understood, but he wasn't sure that he did.

The phone rang, and Jurgens answered. 'What?' And then, after a minute, 'What?' much louder. 'Great!' he yelled. 'Thank you.' He slammed the phone down and vaulted over the desk. 'They've found him,' he informed Marya at the top of his lungs, pulling her up from the bench and starting to do an impromptu jig around the office.

'Where?' Marya demanded.

'In the jungle near a town called Pawa-Tee, it sounded like. A woman was going out early this morning to cut cane or something, and she found him lying on the trail.'

'How is he?'

'They're not sure yet. They'll know better after they examine him. He just arrived at the hospital.'

'Which one?' Marya asked, reaching for her jacket.

'The Southern Baptist Missionary

Hospital in Bonterre — wait a minute, I'll go with you.'

⋆　⋆　⋆

Peter slept for a day before the doctor decided it would be all right for him to wake up. They unfastened the tubes from his arms, took away the bottles of plasma, which he had graduated to from whole blood, and cut off the sedation.

He was staring at an expanse of white. Gradually it came into focus as a hospital ceiling. Then other sensations started to intrude, and he felt the coolness of the sheets he was tucked gently between. Around his body from waist to shoulder he could feel the firm constriction of bandages. Also, it seemed to him, his feet were bandaged, although he couldn't be sure: the feeling might be due to the sheets pulling tight at the base of the bed. He mused on these sensations for a while, then turned his head to look at the rest of the room.

'You're awake!'

Peter focused on the spot the voice had

come from. Marya was sitting on a chair by the side of the bed. She had been reading a magazine, which she let drop when she saw Peter move his head. 'Hi,' Peter said. It was the best he could manage.

'How do you feel?' Marya asked, leaning over.

'I don't,' he said. 'I mean, I can feel the sheets around me, and the bandages, and the breeze on my face, but I don't seem to feel anything from inside.'

'You shouldn't, I guess. There's still enough morphine inside of you to sedate an elephant with a toothache.'

'How long have you been here?' Peter asked.

'Since they brought you in yesterday.'

'Yesterday? Tell me, how am I?'

'The doctor says you're fine. You've lost a lot of blood, but they put most of it back; and the bullets didn't hit anything vital.'

'Bullets? How many?'

'Two. Here,' Marya took a little bottle off the bedside table and shook it in front of Peter, where he could easily see it. Two misshapen pieces of lead jiggled around the bottom of the bottle. 'They took them out of you yesterday afternoon. The whole thing only took about ten minutes.' She put the bottle back on the table. 'You'll probably be able to get up and walk around in about two days, but you won't be doing much for three weeks to a month. The doctor says you were very lucky and the bullets didn't hit any bones or rupture any muscles or anything.' She paused for breath. 'And I'm glad you're all right.'

'You've been sitting there since yesterday?' Peter asked.

'What's wrong with that?' asked Marya defensively.

'Nothing,' Peter assured her, 'I think it's wonderful.'

'Mister Jurgens was here too, but he had to go back to the base. He said to say hello when you woke up. Hello.' She leaned over and kissed him.

'I hope,' Peter said, smiling, 'that the kiss is from you and not Eric.' He rolled over and, happily, went back to sleep.

When Peter woke up again, Marya was

just coming back into his room. 'Have you been here since I went to sleep?' Peter asked, sitting up to look at the clock on the table. He felt much stronger.

'You mean you've been sleeping since I left?' Marya asked. 'I went out to the fort to get some clothing and stuff for you, and I brought Mister Jurgens back with me. He's putting the jeep in the lot, and will be up directly,' she advanced toward the bed, 'which doesn't give us very much time to say hello.'

Peter was happy to discover that he could put his arms around her and hold her tightly with little effort. They stayed like that for some time.

'Ahem.' A pause. 'Maybe I should have knocked.' It was Jurgens' voice. They didn't move. 'I met your father downstairs,' Jurgens continued, 'and he said he'd be right up.'

Marya slowly pushed herself away from Peter and got off the bed.

'Spoilsport,' said Peter.

'Sorry about that,' said a smiling Jurgens. 'I wouldn't have interrupted you two for the world, but I thought you might like to know.'

Marya straightened her hair. 'It isn't that I wouldn't want father to know, but I don't think he'd approve of me attacking a defenseless man.'

'What's that?' Trimam's voice boomed ahead of him, and then he followed it into the room.

'I was just kissing Mister Carthage,' Marya explained.

'Of course you were,' her father said. 'I'm quite aware of your, er, opinion of Mister Carthage. Although I would think you'd wait until he was out of bed and able to defend himself.'

Peter sat up in bed. 'It's good to see you, sir. Although I believe I'm a bit embarrassed.'

'Nonsense,' Trimam brushed the idea aside. 'It's not often that a father approves of his daughter's taste in men as much as he does the young man's taste in women. How do you feel?'

'Healthy, whole, and guilty about taking up a hospital bed,' Peter said.

'You'll be ambulatory tomorrow and out of here by the day after, although you shouldn't be doing much for a couple of weeks. I spoke to your doctor downstairs.'

'Everyone's seen my doctor but me,' Peter commented.

'He's seen a lot of you,' Jurgens told him, 'but you've been unconscious so much of the time that he's never been able to catch you awake. He was rather annoyed about it, too. It seems that there are forms and things to fill out. By rights he shouldn't have operated on you until they had the name and address of your next of kin.'

'I'm glad they didn't wait,' Peter said. 'I had a lot of sleep to catch up on.'

'You're caught up now,' Jurgens said.

'Not quite,' Peter said. 'What's been happening?'

Jurgens sat down at the foot of the bed. 'The strike was a complete success. The only ones who got away went through that tunnel. Of course they took you with them, but that's been remedied. Aside from the prisoners,' Jurgens dismissed the prisoners with a wave of his hand, 'we also got about a quarter-ton of documents. You know, I think the ultimate weapon would be something that makes mimeograph machines break down at a distance. Also, our replacements are here.'

'Our what?' Peter demanded.

'The honorable Mister Steadman,' Jurgens carefully explained, 'has, on careful reading of the weekly reports we've been sending him, decided that Phase One — the creation of training procedures for the Bonterre Army — has been completed; and Phase Two — the continued training of the Army under the established procedures, is ready to commence. We, representing Phase One, are therefore superfluous, and are to remain only long enough for our replacements, representing Phase Two, to get acclimated. That, roughly, is what the letter the Old Man sent along with them said. They landed with a load of communications equipment this morning.'

'Well, at least we're not going home in disgrace,' Peter said.

'Not at all,' Jurgens agreed. 'As a matter of fact, we have one more hit scheduled before we hand over the keys. The General Staff has suddenly come up with a scheme involving Special Forces and three whole Infantry Battalions. It's set for tomorrow morning.'

'Keep 'em on the run,' Peter said, 'I don't suppose — '

'You certainly don't,' Jurgens agreed sternly. 'You're to stay in bed until the doctor says otherwise. Even when you get up, you'll be in no shape to be running around. Don't push your luck.'

'You have a point there. I'll just sit around here quietly and mope. What caused the General Staff to have such a sudden change of heart? Last I heard Motyse and his boys still had enough pull to make them completely ignore us. Did the Prime Minister suddenly fire three or four generals?'

Trimam shook his head. 'Nothing like that, unfortunately. He still doesn't have the political strength. That'll have to wait either until after the next election, or until after the rightists attempt their coup.'

'If they fail,' Peter commented.

'If they fail,' Trimam agreed sadly.

'So why do you think the General Staff suddenly decided to use Special Forces?'

'Who can tell?' Trimam shrugged.

'I figure they're hoping we'll fall flat on our faces,' Jurgens suggested.

'Could be,' Peter agreed. 'Well, be careful and see that you don't.'

Jurgens stood up. 'We'll do our best. Your suitcase is by the bed, with clothes and a toothbrush and things. I even brought you something to read.'

'Thanks,' Peter said. 'What?'

'One of those mystery things. Someone brought it in on the plane this morning.' Jurgens opened the case, and pulled out a book. 'Here.' He tossed it to Peter. *Death of a Doxy*, by Rex Stout.

'Very good,' Peter said. 'One of my favorite authors.'

Jurgens snorted. 'How can you enjoy that stuff? We're in the middle of a war, and you read detective stories.'

'Adventure,' said Peter obscurely, 'is where you aren't. Beside, it's an intellectual exercise, stimulation of the reasoning ability.'

Peter's visitors left the room, and he settled down to read. The nurse brought him dinner, and he was glad to find that he was hungry. He ate well, coaxed the nurse out of a second dessert, and then went back to the adventures of Nero Wolfe, the modern Mycroft.

16

The next morning Peter got up, feeling weak but healthy, took a shower, shaved himself and got dressed. Shortly afterward, while he was lying on top of the bed reading and waiting for his breakfast, a white-coated man came into the room and yelled 'Good morning' cheerfully at him.

Peter looked up from the book. 'Good morning,' he agreed.

'And how are we today?'

'I'm fine, how are you?'

'Fine, fine.' He advanced toward Peter and grabbed his wrist. 'I'm Doctor Pectin,' he said, hunting for Peter's pulse.

'Glad to meet you, Doc. When can I get out of here?'

'Tomorrow morning, I should say. Here, let's look under those bandages and see what kind of job I did on you.' He helped Peter off with his shirt and cut the bandages off the arm and shoulder. He prodded the area with his finger, and Peter winced. 'Hurt?' Doctor Pectin asked.

'A bit, just a bit.'

'That's good. Good sign. Let's wrap it up again.' He opened a package of sterile gauze and started rewrapping the wound. 'You should be able to take the stitches out in a week or so, and in a month you won't know anything ever happened.'

'That's good news,' Peter said.

'You were very lucky.' The doctor finished bandaging the damaged area, and Peter put his shirt back on. There was a sound of running feet in the hall, and then Marya burst into the room. 'Peter.' She paused for breath. 'You've got to . . . do something . . . quick . . . '

'Hold on,' Peter directed. 'Sit down and catch your breath, then tell me what happened. Here, have a glass of water.' He poured water from a pitcher on the table, and watched her gulp it down.

'Thanks,' she said. She paused and breathed deeply for a few seconds.

'This's the young girl who sat up with you the first night you got here,' the doctor identified. 'What's the matter?'

'That's better,' Marya gulped. 'I ran all the way here.'

'From where?' Peter asked.

'From the palace. We have trouble. A group of soldiers have surrounded the building, and General Motyse came in to talk to the King.'

'General Motyse,' Peter said. 'I should have guessed.' He swung his legs over the side of the bed. 'How long ago did this start?'

'About half an hour ago,' Marya told him. 'I got away as soon as I could.'

'How did you manage to get by the soldiers?'

'I've played in the palace since I was five years old. There are a couple of ways to get in and out that aren't easy to spot unless you know them. What do you think is happening, and what do we do about it?'

'I've got a good idea of what's happening,' Peter said, 'but I have to check and make sure. Then we'll figure out what to do about it. I'm sorry, Doctor Pectin, but you're going to have to let me out of here a day earlier than you planned.'

The doctor shrugged. 'If you have to leave, you have to leave. But take it easy.'

'I'll take it as easy as I can,' Peter assured the doctor. He said to Marya, 'Come with me, we'll find out what's going on.'

The two of them left the hospital and walked the six blocks to the parliament building, where the Prime Minister had his office. As they rounded the corner to the street the building was on, Peter stopped and held Marya's arm. 'Look,' he said, indicating the two sets of double doors that were the main entrances. There were two armed soldiers standing at ease before each of the doors. 'That tells us what we want to know. The day of the coup is here.'

'What are we going to do?'

'A good question,' Peter admitted, 'but let's walk while we figure out an answer. We'll be too conspicuous standing here.' He guided Marya around the corner, and they started walking casually down the side street. 'They've taken over the palace and the parliament building,' Peter mused. 'If I were in their shoes, I'd also grab the radio station, police headquarters, the telegraph office and the courthouse. I'd also have a list of people to be arrested. As soon as I got everything under control, I'd announce the success of a bloodless — let us hope — revolution, and the formation of a new government. That's what I'd do. The question is, what can we do about it?' Peter suddenly steered Marya into a doorway.

'What's up?' she asked.

'A squad of soldiers just came around the corner. They're probably looking for the names on that list I mentioned, and that means us.'

Marya sat down on the staircase and looked sadly up at Peter. 'There must be something we can do.'

'There always is,' Peter agreed. 'I can think of several somethings, the question is which is the best.'

'Why did they pick now to attack?' Marya asked.

'Well, probably because of the strike force that went out this morning. The infantry units that went in with Special Forces must have been the ones that

General Motyse thought were too loyal to go along with his scheme. Those left in the city, I'd imagine, are staffed by rightwing officers.'

'Is there any way we can get in touch with Colonel Lyet and have the attack called off, or something?'

Peter looked at his watch. 'It's a quarter past eight, and the attack was scheduled for nine o'clock. If we can get word to them in the next forty-five minutes, there's a chance. Once they've started the attack it would be very difficult to recall them. You know, it occurs to me that there's a real chance that the strike force is flying into a trap — it would be a good way for Motyse to eliminate competition.'

'Can't we radio them?' Marya asked.

'General Motyse must have control of every radio transmitter in the city, and we'd never reach Fort Alpha in time. Wait a minute! Do you remember what Eric was talking about last night?'

'You mean your replacements, what about them?'

'They must be at Fort Alpha by now, but he said they flew in with a load of communications equipment. The odds are good that it's still at the airport warehouse.'

'But it might have been moved already,' Marya said. 'Besides, wouldn't General Motyse have a guard posted at the airport?'

'Probably, but the guard is there to stop any planes from leaving, not to watch the airport warehouse. Anyhow, it's our best chance. We'll just have to hope the equipment is still there. It should be, it's usually a couple of days before they get around to distributing new equipment.'

'How are we going to get out to the airport?' Marya asked.

'I hate to take you along, but you might be able to help,' Peter told her.

'You couldn't get rid of me,' Marya assured him.

'I won't try. Come on, let's get going.'

They left the building. The street was clear of soldiers, and seemed strangely clear of people. When they rounded the corner, they could see why. There was a barricade across the street, and soldiers were checking the identification of everyone who passed.

'Wrong way,' Peter said. 'We'd never make it.'

'What do we do?'

'Well, I had the bright idea of going back to the hospital and borrowing one of their ambulances, but I guess that's out. We'll have to improvise.' They walked along the street, without undue haste, and turned the corner.

'Will they come after us?' asked Marya.

'Not unless they get overly suspicious. What they'll do is cordon off whole areas of the city to prevent movement between, and then send in other groups to conduct a house-to-house search. It's a fairly standardized procedure.' Peter kept walking, his hands thrust deep into his pockets. 'I'm not sure how to get out of this one . . . wait a second!'

'What is it?'

'Look at that.' Peter pointed to an alley next to a cleaner's.

'What about it?'

'I think it's our passport out of here. Come on.' Together, they strolled into the alley.

Five minutes later the cleaner's truck

pulled out of the alley. It was a type of vehicle very common to the streets of Bonterre, a three-wheeled motor scooter, with a closed front cab and a large rear section, this one all taken up by cleaned clothes hanging from a pipe. The truck was driven by a very pretty girl wearing a work-smock, with her hair tied in a large handkerchief. The small truck turned onto the street leading up to the roadblock and stopped. The girl got out, went around to the back, took out a package and went into the nearest building.

The truck made two more stops on that block, the last one right in front of the blockade. Then the girl pulled the truck up to the blockade. 'Hello,' she said to the private who flagged her down, 'what's all this?'

'Just a routine check,' the soldier assured her. 'May I see your papers?'

'Papers?' the girl repeated, wiping her hands on the smock. 'Sure, why not?' She reached down to the seat beside her, and produced a leather wallet. 'Here,' she said, 'my identification card.'

263

The soldier didn't notice as he stared at the card that the girl kept the truck in gear and her foot on the gas. 'Marya,' he said, handing her the card back. 'It's a nice name, Marya. Do you live around here?'

'By the tailor shop on the next block.'

'Are you doing anything this evening?' the soldier asked.

'I'm working until eight o'clock. You can come pick me up at the shop at eight.'

'If I get off at all this evening,' the soldier said glumly. He waved the truck through the blockade.

The truck encountered two more stopping points in its trip to the airport and successfully negotiated both of them, leaving clean clothes in a lot of hallways in the process.

The little scooter truck approached the front gate of the airport. Three guards approached it. 'What do you want?' one of them, a sergeant with a machine gun, asked, waving his gun in the girl's face.

'Hello.' The girl stuck her head out of the window. 'I have to pick up some laundry and deliver clean uniforms.'

'You can't go in,' the sergeant told her.

'Fine,' she assured him. 'Would you take the things in for me, please? They have to be delivered, but I'm sure I can trust you.'

'Well,' the sergeant considered for a minute. 'It would be all right, I suppose, if one of my men goes with you.'

'Very good, Sergeant, thank you.' The truck started forward, and one of the men swung aboard the back and sat on the edge, his feet dangling above the road. After the vehicle had gone through the gate and was swinging around toward the complex of buildings at the end of the runway, a hand reached out from behind the pile of clothes, and grabbed the soldier by the neck. A sudden jerk, and the trooper disappeared into the truck.

A minute later someone knocked on the wall of the cab from inside the truck. 'Okay, he's trussed up like a turkey.'

The cleaning van swung around the administration building and passed several of the outlying structures. It pulled to a stop in front of a large warehouse. An officious guard, one of the Airport Police, not a soldier, trotted up to the van. 'What are you doing here?' the cop asked.

'I have to pick up a load of sheets,' Marya told him.

'You're at the wrong building,' the guard told her. 'I . . . ' That was as far as he got. Peter dropped off the rear of the van, tiptoed behind the guard, and in one motion pulled off the guard's helmet and dotted him on the back of the head. The guard folded up and lay down on the concrete.

Peter picked up the guard by the arms, pulled him through the giant warehouse doors and trussed him up by his own belt. 'That'll do,' he called.

Marya drove the van into the warehouse and got out. 'What next?'

'Close those doors so nobody spots the truck,' Peter directed. 'I'll see if I can find those radios.' He started walking down the wide aisles of the warehouse, checking the markings on the crates. When Marya had got the doors closed, she went back to find Peter wrestling one of the crates free from the top of a huge pile, twelve feet above the floor.

'Be careful,' she called, 'that whole stack's going to collapse.'

'I've got it,' Peter said, pulling the box loose. 'Now the only problem is getting it down. I'll need both hands to climb off this pile.'

'Can't you hand it down to me?' Marya asked.

'I guess that's what I'll have to do.' Peter carefully lay down on his stomach and worked the crate around. He lowered it down toward Marya, who stretched her hands up to reach it. 'Be careful — it must weigh sixty pounds.'

'I can't quite reach it,' Marya said, straining upward.

'Climb up on a couple of those boxes,' Peter suggested.

'All right.' Marya went around to the side of the pile and clambered up on a large crate. 'Can you get it around?'

'Hope so.' Peter swung the box over to the side as far as he could.

'I've got it!' Marya announced. 'You can let go.'

Peter slowly let go of the box. Marya

almost fell over forward, but managed to stop in time.

'Don't try to get down with that,' Peter said. 'Here, wait a second.' He jumped off the pile of crates, wincing as the shock of landing ran up to his shoulder. 'Okay, now hand it to me.'

Marya tried to swing the box down from where it was balanced over her head, but it proved too heavy for her. At the last instant she dropped it. Peter caught it in his arms, and went staggering backward. 'Oh,' Marya gasped. 'I'm sorry, I couldn't hold it.'

'That's all right,' Peter told her from where he sat on the floor, 'I don't love you for your weight-lifting ability.'

'Oh,' Marya said in a small voice. She jumped down from the crate. 'Do you love me?'

'We'd better discuss it later,' Peter said. He pulled at the top of the crate. 'I can't get this board loose.'

'Here,' Marya said, handing him a crowbar, 'I found this up by the door. I thought you might need it.'

Peter paused to look at her. 'Most

men,' he informed her, 'don't like women who are smarter than they are. Lucky for you I'm not most men.' He pulled Marya down and kissed her.

He took the crowbar and pried open the case. 'Here they are,' he said, pulling a metallic-gray box free of the case and setting it on the floor. 'A command radio transceiver.' He stared at the dials on the front panel for a moment, and then clicked a switch. 'Hell,' he said after a short pause.

'What's the matter?'

'It doesn't work.' He stared at it for a minute, and then snapped his fingers. 'Of course.' He turned the set around, and opened a small door at the rear. 'Empty. No batteries. They must have been sent separately.' Peter got up off the floor, and started scanning the cases. 'They must be around here somewhere.'

'What's this?' Marya asked, pulling a square brown object out of the open case.

'That's it,' Peter said. 'The battery. You've done it again.' He took it and plugged it into its receptacle. 'Now, one more thing.' He fished around in the case until he came up with what looked like a collapsed fishing pole.

'What do you have there?' Marya asked.

'The whip antenna,' Peter told her. He screwed the sections together until it was about fifteen feet long, and then plugged it in to a hole on top of the set.

'Here we go,' he said.

17

'Five minutes to the drop zone,' the pilot announced.

Jurgens crouched by the door of the transport helicopter and watched the jungle flow by beneath him.

'Colonel Jurgens, will you please come forward,' the pilot called over the intercom. He sounded puzzled.

Jurgens pulled himself up and threaded his way down the thin aisle, past the two rows of combat-ready soldiers. He reached the front, and clambered up the ladder to the pilot's compartment. 'What is it?'

'We're getting something funny over the radio,' the pilot told him. 'Listen.' The pilot pulled his earphones off and handed them to Jurgens, who held one up to his ear.

'*Peter Carthage calling Colonel Lyet or Eric Jurgens. Emergency, please reply.*' Pause. '*Peter Carthage calling Colonel Lyet or Eric Jurgens. Emergency, please reply.*'

Pause. '*Peter* . . .'

'How long has this been coming in?' Jurgens asked.

'We called you when it started.'

'Hand me the microphone.'

'We're under strict orders to maintain radio silence,' the pilot protested.

'How far to the zone?' Jurgens asked.

'About a minute now.'

'Give me that microphone,' Jurgens growled. 'That's Carthage, I recognize his voice.'

'Why doesn't he use the call signs?' the pilot demanded.

'He doesn't know them. I'll take the responsibility.' He grabbed the microphone. 'Is it on transmit?'

The pilot flipped a switch. 'It is now. Just push the button on the mike and talk.'

Jurgens waited until the next pause in the repeated call, and pushed the button. 'Jurgens here.'

'Eric? Thank God. Have you landed yet?'

'No.'

'Don't. It's probably a trap. You're needed here.'

'Drop zone in sight,' the pilot's voice sang out.

'Don't land,' Jurgens ordered. 'Circle it for a minute. Notify the other copters.'

The pilot relayed the order with his throat mike on the pilot-to-pilot frequency, while Jurgens stayed on the command radio. Peter's tinny voice came over the earphones describing the situation in the capital city.

'We'll see what we can do,' Jurgens said. 'Take care of yourself, you shouldn't be out of bed.' He signed off.

'Let's get out of here,' Jurgens told the pilot. 'Head for the capital.'

The helicopters lifted from the field they'd been circling and pulled away. As they did, camouflage nets were pulled aside from machine-gun emplacements around the field, and the dug-in guerrillas started firing at the helicopters. Jurgens, peering through a window in the cockpit, saw one of the guerrillas standing by a gun emplacement and shaking his fist at the retreating copters.

'Look at him,' Jurgens said, pointing the man out to the pilot, 'he seems annoyed at something.'

'It's a good thing we didn't land,' the pilot said.

'You could say that,' Jurgens agreed.

18

'After that,' Jurgens explained, 'it was simple. When twelve troop-carrying helicopters landed on the lawn behind the palace, the group holding King Min gave up without a shot. Well, almost without a shot. General Motyse put a bullet through his own head before we could get to him.'

They were sitting in the living room of Professor Perlemutter's hotel suite. Peter had just come in from the airport in the helicopter Jurgens had sent for him, and Ambassador Trimam had taken Marya home with him.

'What about the other rightist troops?' Peter asked.

'You know the jeep we had fitted out with an overhead bar to stand up and review troops in?'

Peter nodded.

'Well, with Colonel Lyet driving and the King standing up in back, we went around to all the strongpoints the rightists had grabbed. I followed up behind with a couple of trucks full of men, but they weren't needed. When they saw the King coming, they all surrendered. I guess that two thousand years of tradition can be helpful at times.'

'As simple as that,' Peter said.

'It wouldn't have been if you hadn't gotten to us in time. Give Motyse a day or two holding the King incommunicado to consolidate his position, and the government would have fallen. By then it would have been too late to do anything.'

The door to the bedroom opened, and Professor Perlemutter came stomping out into the living room waving a paper in front of him. 'Here's an example of unbiased reporting for you. Bah!'

'What's that?' Peter asked.

'Our friend Logan's latest report home. We read them as fast as he sends them now.'

'What's he have to say?' Jurgens asked.

'Here, read it.' Perlemutter put the paper down on the desk between them, and they both bent over to read.

ANTI-COMMUNIST FORCES IN THE BONTERRE GOVERNMENT ATTEMPTED

TO OVERTHROW THE QUOTE NEUTRAL UNQUOTE GOVERNMENT HERE TODAY STOP WITH THE AID OF WAR INC TRAINED TROOPS PRIME MINISTER AGAIN WAS ABLE TO QUASH THE COUP ATTEMPT STOP DETAILS TO FOLLOW STOP LOGAN

'He doesn't have all the facts yet,' Perlemutter said, 'but he'll be sending them along directly. With his own patent built-in bias.'

'Are all his reports like this?' Peter asked.

'There's a certain tendency evident in all of them,' Perlemutter said. 'Here, wait a moment.' He disappeared into the bedroom, and came out with a thick folder. 'Look through them yourself.'

Peter took the folder and leafed through it. He paused at one of the reports and read it carefully through. Then he took it out of the folder and put it in his inside pocket. 'You know,' he said, 'I think we might be able to clear up this business once and for all.'

'What business?' Jurgens asked.

'The mysterious leader of the rightists

277

and their relationship with the guerrillas. That is, if I'm right.' He stood up. 'Come along with me, and let's find out.'

'Fine,' Jurgens said. 'Where are we going?'

'We're going to pick up Colonel Lyet and his squad of intelligence men and search a house.'

Three hours later four jeeps pulled up in front of the DuMarte Plantation main house. Peter, Jurgens and Colonel Lyet climbed out of the lead jeep and started up the porch stairs. Before they had reached the top, Mme. DuMarte came out to greet them.

'Gentlemen,' she said, advancing toward them, 'to what do I owe this unexpected visit?'

Colonel Lyet pulled a folded document out of his pocket and handed it to her.

'Why, Colonel, what is this?'

'An order for us to search your house and grounds, Madame. I regret the necessity, and will inconvenience you as little as possible.' He touched his hand to the brim of his hat, turned around, and barked orders to the men in the other jeeps.

'But surely this isn't necessary,' Annette

DuMarte protested. 'Of course you and your men can feel free to look anywhere you like. If you'll tell me what you're looking for, perhaps I can help you.'

'We're looking for a still, Madame,' Peter said, not feeling very happy.

'A still?'

'A distillation plant. Specifically one being used to process raw opium into heroin.'

Colonel Lyet's men spread out, some of them going past the group on the porch and into the great house, and others to the various smaller houses on the plantation.

'Why do you think you'll find such a device here?' Madame DuMarte asked lightly. 'Surely if it were I'd know about it.'

'That's true, Madame,' Colonel Lyet said. He went into the house with Jurgens, leaving Peter alone with Madame DuMarte.

'Peter.' Annette came over to him and put her hand on his arm. 'What does this mean?'

'It means you played me for a sucker,' Peter told her severely, 'but I caught on. It's as simple as that.'

'How can you say that, Peter?' Annette's eyes widened as she looked at him.

279

'Don't play the sweet innocent role,' Peter told her. 'It's too late. I know damned well who you are and what you've been doing.'

'What do you mean, who I am?'

'The guerrillas know you as X,' Peter said. 'You're the supply source for guns and ammunition.'

'And why have I been doing this?' Annette demanded, 'part of some right-wing plot to undermine the government?'

'That's probably part of it. But mainly in return for raw opium. Here, look at this.' He handed her the paper he had put in his pocket back in the hotel room. It was a report from Logan, dated several months before. Part of it read:

ONE OF THE LEADERS OF THE ANTI-COMMUNIST GROUP HERE IS A MADAME ANNETTE DUMARTE STOP HER PLANTATION IS BEING USED TO SMUGGLE IN SUPPLIES FOR THE PROJECTED COUP STOP THIS EXPLAINS REPORTS MADE PREVIOUSLY ABOUT ACTIVITY AFTER DARK OF SMALL BOATS IN AREA STOP

'How'd you sell him on that explanation of the boats?' Peter asked bitterly. 'The same way you got me to stop looking over that cabin cruiser? What were you afraid I'd find in that forward locker I never got to — the opium crates?'

'This is ridiculous,' Annette snapped. 'I don't have to listen to any of it.' She brushed by him, and started down the stairs.

Peter grabbed her arm, and she froze. For a minute they stood like that, neither of them moving.

The tableau was broken by Colonel Lyet, who came to the door of the house. 'It's in the basement,' he said, 'behind a false wall. If my men weren't trained searchers, they never would have found it. There must be thirty pounds of unprocessed opium in that room.'

Annette turned to face Peter. 'It could have been so different,' she said softly. With her free hand, she raked her nails down the side of his face, leaving four deep red welts.

★   ★   ★

Peter rode glumly up the hotel elevator toward the room he was occupying for his last days in Bonterre. John Little, War, Inc.'s second-string quarterback, had taken over Peter's office and quarters at Fort Alpha. The Royal banquet had been last night, and the official thank-yous and goodbyes had all been said. All that was left was the leaving. The jet was sitting there waiting to take him back to his desk job tomorrow morning.

Everyone else, Peter reflected, turning the key in the lock, had found something to do on this last night. He felt guilty being there at all. After all, how many times can you say goodbye? And, in the unkindest cut of all, Marya had disappeared for the last two days.

When he closed the door behind him, he couldn't figure out what was wrong with the room. It took him a second to realize that the shower in the bathroom was running.

'Is that you?' a voice called out. The shower was turned off. Then Marya came out of the bathroom, a large towel wrapped around her. 'Hello,' she said.

'Your mouth's open.'

Feeling suddenly weak, Peter sat on the edge of the bed. 'What are you doing here?'

'You're leaving tomorrow morning?' Marya asked.

'That's right.'

'I've been visiting an aunt in the country for two days — my mother's idea. I'm supposed to be there another two days. I came back to say goodbye to you properly.'

She released the tuck that held the towel around her.

We do hope that you have enjoyed reading this large print book.

Did you know that all of our titles are available for purchase?

We publish a wide range of high quality large print books including:
Romances, Mysteries, Classics
General Fiction
Non Fiction and Westerns

Special interest titles available in large print are:
The Little Oxford Dictionary
Music Book, Song Book
Hymn Book, Service Book

Also available from us courtesy of Oxford University Press:
Young Readers' Dictionary
(large print edition)
Young Readers' Thesaurus
(large print edition)

For further information or a free brochure, please contact us at:
Ulverscroft Large Print Books Ltd.,
The Green, Bradgate Road, Anstey,
Leicester, LE7 7FU, England.
Tel: (00 44) **0116 236 4325**
Fax: (00 44) **0116 234 0205**

THE COMIC BOOK KILLER

Richard A. Lupoff

Hobart Lindsey is a quiet man, a bachelor living with his widowed mother in the suburbs and working as an insurance claims agent. Marvia Plum is a tough, savvy, street-smart cop. Then fate throws the unlikely pair together. A burglary at a vintage comic book store leads to a huge insurance claim that Lindsey must investigate for his company — and to the brutal murder of the store owner, for which Marvia must find the killer. Lindsey and Plum, like oil and water — but working together to unravel a baffling mystery!

THE GREEN PEN MYSTERY

Donald Stuart

Caught in a thunderstorm one hot summer night, Peter Lake takes shelter in a public call-box. When the telephone begins to ring, and curiosity prompts him to answer, a desperate plea for help issues from the receiver — then a scream — then silence. His determination to assist the owner of the mystery voice will fling him headlong into uncharted seas of crime, danger and sudden death . . . Meanwhile, Adam Kane, brilliant and unorthodox solicitor, brings his powerful intellect to bear on four baffling cases.

THE POSTBOX MURDERS

Edmund Glasby

Chief Inspector James Holbrooke and the police are utterly baffled by the terrifying activities of the Postbox Killer, an apparent madman who is butchering his victims and stuffing them into village postboxes. It is left to eccentric private investigator Richard Montrose to uncover the killer — and the astonishing reason for his grisly actions . . . While in *Death After Death*, a man is plagued by nightmares and bodily horrors that disappear as inexplicably as they appear. Is he going mad? Or is there another, more macabre explanation?

A CORNISH OBSESSION

Rena George

It's a snowy December night in Marazion, and Jago Tilley is making his unsteady way home from the village pub. By morning, he will be dead . . . Investigating the brutal murder is DI Sam Kitto — and, once again, his magazine editor girlfriend Loveday Ross finds herself involved in the case. Suspicion falls on several people — the dead man's disreputable nephew; an arrogant art dealer; and a glamorous boutique owner. Meanwhile, Loveday's boss is acting distinctly out of character . . .